"You're a...woman?"

In a breathless whisper, she said, "You just now noticed that? Could you let me breathe?"

Shocked, he shifted his weight to allow her to take breath into her lungs. This was the cat burglar?

She freed one arm and wiped away the powdery snow from her eyes as she whispered something else.

He cut his eyes to her, suddenly worried that he had injured her when he'd taken her down. She motioned for him to lean closer. He bent down.

Her free hand cupped the back of his neck, pulling him down into a kiss before he could stop her. Suddenly her lips were on his, her mouth parting as if they were lovers...

REUNION AT CARDWELL RANCH

New York Times Bestselling Author

B.J. DANIELS

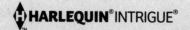
HARLEQUIN® INTRIGUE®

There are books that seem to write themselves. And there are
books that try to kill me. This one drove me crazy. But thanks to
an escape to the Bahamas with people I love, I was able to finish
the book. This one is for Danielle, Travis, Stelly, Leslie and,
always, Parker. Your faith in me keeps me going.

ISBN-13: 978-0-373-69878-3

Reunion at Cardwell Ranch

Copyright © 2016 by Barbara Heinlein

Recycling programs
for this product may
not exist in your area.

Printed in U.S.A.

www.Harlequin.com

B.J. Daniels is a *New York Times* and *USA TODAY* bestselling author. She wrote her first book after a career as an award-winning newspaper journalist and the publication of thirty-seven short stories. She lives in Montana with her husband, Parker, and three springer spaniels. When not writing, she quilts, boats and plays tennis. Contact her at bjdaniels.com, on Facebook or on Twitter, @bjdanielsauthor.

Books by B.J. Daniels

Harlequin Intrigue

Cardwell Cousins

Rescue at Cardwell Ranch
Wedding at Cardwell Ranch
Deliverance at Cardwell Ranch
Reunion at Cardwell Ranch

Crime Scene at Cardwell Ranch
Justice at Cardwell Ranch
Cardwell Ranch Trespasser
Christmas at Cardwell Ranch

HQN Books

The Montana Hamiltons

Wild Horses
Lone Rider
Lucky Shot

Visit the Author Profile page at Harlequin.com for more titles.

CAST OF CHARACTERS

Laramie Cardwell—The Texas cowboy only planned to spend the Christmas holidays in Montana with his family. But that was before he had a run-in with a female cat burglar.

Obsidian "Sid" Forester—The artist and thief can't let anyone stop her—even a handsome Texas cowboy who is determined to capture her.

Zander Andrews—She'd made a lot of mistakes when it came to what little family she had left. Did she dare hope that this Christmas could change all that?

Taylor West—The cowboy artist thought he had it all, a young wife and a promising career—until his wife ran off and Laramie Cardwell showed up at his door.

Rock Jackson—The artist's love for women was costing him after two divorces, but he'd found a way to have it all.

Hank Ramsey—He and three others had started the Old West Artists' Coalition to promote themselves and cowboy art, but maybe they'd been too restrictive about who they let into their club.

Cody Kentworth—The artist knew he was only as good as his reputation.

Dana Cardwell Savage—Her Christmas wish was to get the last of her Cardwell cousins to Montana.

Chapter One

The moment she'd stepped into the dark house, she could feel the emptiness surround her like a void. The owners wouldn't be coming to Montana for Christmas this year. The couple was getting a divorce. The man's third marriage, the woman's first.

She'd gotten her information from a good source, but she'd learned, though, that you can never be certain of anything, especially the rumors that ran more wildly than the river ran through the Gallatin Canyon past Big Sky.

Standing stone still in the dark, listening, she waited for a few moments before she snapped on her tiny penlight. There were no other homes close to this one. The owners of these expensive spacious second homes wanted to feel as if they had the mountainside to themselves. Because of that there was little to no chance that anyone would notice if she turned on lights. But she didn't like playing against the odds when it came to the chance of being discovered.

As she moved through the house, she saw sculptures that she knew had cost a small fortune and paintings like some she'd sat for hours studying in museums back East. She hurried on past them, reminded that time was never on her side. In and out as quickly as possible was her personal motto. Otherwise she knew all too well things could go very badly.

She found the painting in the master bedroom on the third floor. A twenty-by-sixteen-inch signed Taylor West original depicting a rancher on horseback surveying his herd. It was one of her favorites. She stepped to it quickly, admiring the brushstrokes and the skillful use of shading as she let the penlight move over it until she found what she was looking for.

Lifting it off the wall, she checked the time. She was running a little over five minutes on this job because of the three stories she'd had to search for this piece.

Quickly she replaced the painting with the one she'd brought, noticing that the bag she'd carried it in had torn. Wadding up the bag, she stuffed it into her coat pocket and tucked the painting from the wall under her arm.

She made her way back through the house, pleased. If only they were all as easy as this one. She'd barely completed the thought when a set of headlights washed over the room.

LARAMIE CARDWELL MENTALLY kicked himself for driving up this snow-packed narrow mountain road in the dark. But according to his sister-in-law, and the real-estate agent for the property, if he wanted a house in the Big Sky area, he had to jump on it the moment it became available.

"Why would you want to buy a house up here when you can stay in one of our guesthouses on the ranch whenever you come?" his cousin Dana Cardwell Savage had argued.

While he appreciated her hospitality at Cardwell Ranch, as much time as he found himself spending in Montana, he wanted a place of his own. It had been family that had brought his brothers back to Montana. But it was love—and barbecue—that had them staying.

He often marveled that it had all started with barbecue—the one thing all five brothers knew. They'd opened a small barbecue joint outside of Houston. Surprisingly, it had taken off and they'd opened others, turning a backyard barbecue into a multimillion-dollar business. It had been his brother Tanner "Tag" Cardwell who'd first come up with the idea of opening their first Texas Boys Barbecue restaurant in Montana in Big Sky.

While some of them had balked at the idea, it had proved to be a good one. Now his brothers were talking about opening others in the state. His four brothers had all returned to their Montana roots, but Laramie was a Texas boy who told himself that he had no desire to live in this wild country—at least not full-time.

With his entire family here now, he wanted his own place, and he could darn sure afford a second home. Though he suspected the one he was on his way to check out would be too large for what he needed.

But there was one way to find out. He figured he'd get a look at the house from the outside. If it wasn't what he wanted, then he wouldn't waste his sister-in-law McKenzie's time looking at the interior.

As he topped a small rise in the road, a moonlit Lone Mountain, the peak that dominated Big Sky, appeared from behind a cloud, making him catch his breath. He'd seen the view numerous times on his other visits to the area, but it still captivated him.

He had to admit this part of Montana was spectac-
ular, although he wasn't so sure about staying up here
for the winter. While the snow was awe inspiring in its
beauty, he still wasn't used to the bracing cold up here.

"You wouldn't mind it if you had someone to cud-
dle with at night," his brother Tag had joked. All four
of his brothers had fallen in love in Montana—and
with Montana—and now had wives to snuggle up to
on these cold winter nights.

"I only want a house up here," Laramie had said.
"I can kick up the heat when I spend time here during the holidays."

As he topped the rise in the road, his headlights
caught on a three-story house set against the mountainside. Laramie let up on the gas, captivated by the
design of the house and the way it seemed to belong
on the side of the mountain in the pines.

That's when he spotted the dark figure running
along the roofline of the attached garage.

Chapter Two

Laramie remembered hearing that an alleged cat burglar had been seen in Big Sky, but so far the thief hadn't gotten away with anything.

Until now.

Slamming on the brakes, he threw open the door of his rented SUV, leaped out and took off running. It crossed his mind that the robber might be armed and dangerous. But all he could think about was catching the thief.

The freezing snowy night air made his lungs ache. Even though he'd been the business end of Texas Boys Barbecue, he'd stayed in shape. But he felt the high altitude quicken his breathing and reminded himself he wasn't in Houston anymore.

The dark figure had reached the end of the roofline and now leaped down as agile as any cat he'd ever seen. The thief was dressed in all black including a mask that hid his face. He was carrying what appeared to be a painting.

Laramie tackled the burglar, instantly recognizing his physical advantage. The burglar let out a breath as they hit the ground. The painting skidded across the snow.

Rolling over on top of the thief, Laramie held him down with his weight as he fumbled for his cell phone. The slightly built burglar wriggled under him in the deep snow.

"Hold still," he ordered as he finally got his cell phone out and with freezing fingers began to call his cousin's husband, Marshal Hud Savage.

"You're crushing me."

At the burglar's distinctly female voice, Laramie froze. His gaze cut from the phone to the burglar's eyes—the only exposed part of her face other than her mouth. The eyes were a pale blue in the snowy starlight. "You're a…*woman*?"

In a breathless whisper, she said, "You just now noticed that? Could you let me breathe?"

Shocked, he shifted his weight to allow her to take breath into her lungs. This was the cat burglar?

She freed one arm and wiped away the powdery snow from her eyes as she whispered something else.

He cut his eyes to her, suddenly worried that he had injured her when he'd taken her down. She motioned for him to lean closer. He bent down.

Her free hand cupped the back of his neck, pulling him down into a kiss before he could stop her. Suddenly her lips were on his, her mouth parting as if they were lovers.

The next thing he knew he was lying on his back in the snow looking up at the stars as the cat burglar took off. Her escape had been as much of a surprise as the kiss. He quickly sat up. He'd lost his cell phone and his Stetson. Both had fallen into the snow. He plucked them up as he lumbered to his feet. But by then she was already dropping over the side of the ridge.

He took off after her, but he had gone only a few yards when he heard the roar of a snowmobile engine.

Scrambling after her, he turned the corner of the house in time to see the snowmobile roar off through the snow-heavy pines and disappear. He listened to her get away, feeling like a fool. He'd let her trick him.

She'd taken advantage of his surprise and the extra space he'd given her to breathe. She was a lot stronger and more agile than she had appeared and she had a weapon—those lips. He groaned when he thought about the kiss—and its effects on him.

As he turned back, he saw a corner of the painting sticking up out of the snow. Laramie trudged to where it had landed. The only good news was that she hadn't gotten away with the painting.

Surprisingly the frame was still intact. He carefully brushed away the snow, thinking about the woman who'd gotten away. He'd known his share of women in his life. A few had tempted him, a couple had played havoc with his heart and several had taken him for a ride.

However, none of them had tricked him like this. He could well imagine what his brothers would say.

But would he be able to recognize her if he ever saw her again? She'd never spoken above a whisper and he hadn't gotten a chance to remove her ski mask before she'd dumped him in the snow.

Those eyes. Those lips. He told himself if he ever saw either again, damn straight he'd recognize her.

She thought she was smarter than he. She thought she'd gotten away. But he had the painting. And he would find her—if she didn't find him first, he thought, glancing at the painting in the moonlight.

To the fading sound of the snowmobile, he walked back to his rental SUV. Placing the painting in the backseat, he called his cousin's husband, the marshal.

THAT HAD BEEN too close. As Obsidian "Sid" Forester pulled the snowmobile around to the back of the cabin, she glanced over her shoulder. No headlights. No lights at all. She hadn't been followed.

She'd taken a longer route through the trees. At first she'd thought the man who'd tackled her was the owner of the house. But she'd done her research on him and knew he was much older than the man she'd just encountered.

So who was that cowboy with the Southern drawl? Moonlight on snow did strange things to one's vision. But she had gotten a good look at him—a better look than he'd gotten of her, she assured herself. Thick dark hair. Ice-cold blue eyes. Handsome, if you liked that clean-cut, all-business kind of man. She did not.

The only thing that had thrown her was his accent. Definitely from down South. Definitely not the New Yorker who owned the house.

That wasn't all that had thrown her, she had to admit. The kiss. It had worked just as she'd planned and yet… She touched her tongue to her upper lip, remembering the electrical shock she'd felt when they kissed. Worse was the tingling she'd felt in her belly. True, she hadn't kissed a man in… She couldn't even remember when, but she'd never had that kind of reaction. She certainly hadn't expected to feel…anything.

Her pulse was back to normal by the time she entered the cabin. The air smelled of oil paint, turpentine and linseed oil. She shrugged out of her boots and coat at the back door, hung up her coat and kicked her boots aside as she moved to the painting she'd been working on earlier that day.

She gave it a critical perusal before moving into the small kitchen. Unfortunately she hadn't been to the grocery store in several days. She was always starved after one of what she called her "night jobs." With a bottle of beer—her last—a chunk of cheese and some stale bread, she stepped into the living area where a half dozen paintings were drying.

The cabin was small with only a living room, kitchen, bedroom, small bath and a storage room off to one side at the back. The moment the owner had shown it to her—and told her about all its peculiarities—she'd had to have it and had quickly signed the papers.

Sitting down now, she considered each of her paintings as she ate her snack and sipped her beer. It was hard to concentrate after what had happened earlier, though. She'd come close to getting caught before, but nothing like tonight. What would the man do?

Go to the marshal.

She considered that and decided she wasn't worried about the law catching up with her.

What did worry her was that he had the painting.

Taking another bite of cheese and bread, she chewed for a moment before washing it down with the last of the beer. She really did have to go to the store tomorrow.

Just the thought of going out in public made her wonder if she would run into him. That was the other thing about her cabin. It was nestled in the woods, far from urban Big Sky.

What if she did see him again? She had no doubt

that she would recognize him. She'd gotten a good look at him. He had high cheekbones, a patrician nose and generous mouth. She felt that ridiculous stirring again over that one stupid kiss.

She assured herself that there wasn't any way he could recognize her since she'd had the black ski mask on the whole time. Nor could he recognize her voice since she hadn't spoken above a whisper.

Shaking her head, she tried to put him out of her mind. There was more than a good chance that she would never see him again. Obviously he was a tourist, probably only here for the holidays. Once the holidays were over, he'd be on a jet back to wherever he'd picked up that Southern drawl.

Still, she wondered who he was and why he'd driven up to the house tonight. Probably lost. Just her luck. What other reason could he have had to be there?

But while she'd gotten away, it hadn't been clean, which upset her more than she wanted to admit. She prided herself on her larceny skills. Worse, she'd failed. She didn't have the painting.

Losing her appetite, she tossed the crust of stale bread in the trash and put the cheese back into the fridge before she returned to her work in progress. She always did her best thinking while she painted.

"So, you didn't see her face?" Marshal Hud Savage asked as he looked up from his report at the marshal's office later that night.

"She was wearing a ski mask with only the eyes and mouth part open. Her eyes were this amazing... bluish-silvery color." Laramie frowned. "Maybe it was the starlight but they seemed to change color." He re-alized the marshal was staring at him. "Just put down blue. If I ever see those eyes again, I'll recognize her." Or those lips, he thought, but he wasn't about to tell Hud about the kiss.

It had taken him by surprise—just as she'd planned. But for a moment, his mouth had been on hers. He'd looked into her eyes, felt something quicken inside him, then her warm breath on his cheek and…

He shook his head, reminding himself that it had only been a ploy and he'd fallen for it, hook, line and sinker. He'd kissed a *thief*! What annoyed him was that he had felt anything but disgust for what she'd done.

"How about height and weight?" Hud asked after writing down *blue*.

Laramie shrugged. "Small. Maybe five-five or -six. I have no idea on weight. Slim. I'm sorry I don't have a better description. It all happened too fast. But I have the painting. Maybe you can get her fingerprints—"

"Was she wearing gloves?"

He groaned.

"And you say she got away on a snowmobile?"

All he could do was nod.

"Did you get a make or model?"

Another shake of his head.

"And she overpowered you? Was she armed?"

Laramie groaned inwardly. "Not armed exactly. She was much stronger than I expected and she moved so fast… She caught me off guard."

Hud nodded, but he appeared to be trying hard not to laugh.

"You wait until you find her. She's…wily."

Hud did chuckle then. "I'm sure she is. Here. Sign this."

"So what are the chances you'll catch her?" Laramie asked as he signed the report.

"With a description like the one you just gave me…" Hud shook his head. His phone rang and he reached for it. "Marshal Savage." He listened, his gaze going to Laramie. "Okay. Yep, that'll do it." Hanging up, he picked up the signed report and ripped it in half before tossing it into the trash.

"What?" Laramie demanded.

"I just spoke with the owner of the house. He hadn't planned to come up this holiday, but apparently McKenzie called him yesterday and told him you would be looking at the house. Seems he's anxious to sell, so he flew in tonight." Hud met his gaze. "When I called the maintenance service and asked them to check the house, they found him there. He looked around to see what was missing and found nothing out of order."

"There wasn't anything missing? Was he sure?"

"It seems he has a painting, just like that one…" He pointed to the one leaning against the wall on the floor near Laramie, the painting the cat burglar had dropped. "It isn't missing."

"That's not possible."

Hud shrugged. "The owner says he has the original—the only one of its kind. Also, he said his house hasn't been broken into."

"That can't be right. I saw her coming out of the house."

"Or did you just see her on the ridge of the garage roofline?" the marshal asked.

Laramie thought back. "Maybe I didn't see her come out of the house."

"Since the first report we received about a cat burglar, we've had several sightings. But in all three cases, nothing was taken, the house showed no sign of forced entry…"

Laramie could see where this was going. "So it was a…hoax?"

Hud studied him openly for a moment. "You didn't happen to mention to your brothers that you were going up to that house tonight, did you? They also didn't happen to tell you beforehand about a cat burglar in the area, did they?"

He would kill his brothers. "You think it was a setup?"

Hud shrugged. "You know your brothers better than I do, but I'd say you've been had."

Had in more ways than the marshal could even imagine. He got to his feet. "I'm sorry to bother you with this, then. I just hope they haven't planted counterfeit money on me, as well." His brothers had told him that Hud was investigating a counterfeit operation that had been passing fraudulent money in the canyon.

"Let's hope not," Hud said with a groan. "I get a call a day about a bad twenty. Someone's churning them out," he said getting to his feet. "In the old days it took a lot of expensive equipment and space along with some talent. Now, all you need is a good copy machine. A video online will walk you through the entire process. The good news is that these operations are often small. We aren't talking millions of dollars. Just someone needing some instant spending money."

"Well, good luck finding your counterfeiter and, again, I'm sorry about this. You have enough going on." But as he turned to the door, he said, "What about the painting?"

"The owner swears he has the authenticated original with paperwork on the back." Hud shrugged. "I would imagine this is nothing more than a cheap prop."

"Then you don't mind if I keep it?" Laramie asked.

The marshal chuckled. "It's all yours."

Laramie considered the painting on the floor. It was what he would have called Old West art, a rancher on horseback surveying his herd. It was titled "On The Ranch" and signed by an artist named Taylor West. The painting looked expensive to him, but what did he know?

"If someone comes looking for it, I'll let you know. But I have my doubts." Hud grinned. "If you ever see that woman again, though… I'd be curious just what color her eyes are since they seem to have made a real impression on you."

"REALLY?" LARAMIE DEMANDED when he saw his brother Tanner "Tag" Cardwell at his house the next morning. "That wasn't funny what you and the others pulled last night." He couldn't help but wonder if the kiss had been planned, as well. It was a nice touch, something that would have had his brothers rolling on the floor laughing. "Hud got a real kick out of it since he has nothing to do but take bogus crime reports. I hope he arrests the whole bunch of you."

"I don't know what you're talking about," Tag said as he poured coffee for them.

Laramie looked to his sister-in-law and real-estate agent McKenzie. He'd been staying with them this holiday and, while he enjoyed being with them, he was anxious to get his own place. McKenzie had been helping him find a house.

"Tell me you weren't in on it, too," he said to her.

"I abhor practical jokes." McKenzie shot a disapproving glance at her husband. "What did you and your brothers do?"

"*Nothing. Honest.* I have no idea what he's talking about," Tag said holding up his hands. He looked genuinely innocent.

But Laramie wasn't buying it. He knew his brothers too well. They'd all treated him as if he was the bookworm who ran their family business, Texas Boys Barbecue. They would all have said he was the brother who never had enough adventure in his life.

So it would be just like them to set this up to add some spice to his life, as they would call it.

"Who was the woman?" Laramie demanded.

"There was a *woman*?" Tag asked and grinned.

McKenzie shook her head. "You'll have to tell me about it on the way to the house, Laramie. I promised the owner we'd be there by nine. You can deal with your brothers later."

On the way up the mountain, he told McKenzie about what had happened last night.

"That doesn't sound like something Tag would do," she said. "Are you sure your brothers were behind it?"

"It's the only thing that makes any sense. I saw her leaving with a painting. So, of course, I thought she'd stolen it. I guess that's what I was supposed to think."

"Are you sure the painting you have is a fake?"

"It doesn't look like it to me, but I'm no expert by any means. The owner says he still has the original. So maybe I stopped the woman before she could make the switch, but I could have sworn she was coming *from* the house."

McKenzie seemed to give it some thought. "Maybe she saw your headlights coming up the road and took off before she could make the switch."

"I suppose. If she really was a cat burglar. Or it could be just what the marshal thinks it is—my brothers' idea of a joke.

"I know an art expert if you're interested in finding out about the painting. Or, if it is by a local Western artist, you could take it right to the source," she said.

"Have you ever heard of Taylor West?"

McKenzie looked over at him in surprise. "He's a well-known artist in these parts. He lives farther up the canyon near Taylor Fork. I'm sure if you took the painting to him, he'd be able to tell you if it was his or not."

"I just might do that." He looked up the mountain road ahead and thought about what he'd seen last night as he'd come over the last rise. He couldn't help thinking about the woman. She'd certainly played her part well. If his brothers had been in on it.

He thought about what he'd seen in her eyes just before he started to call the marshal. She'd looked scared. But that could have been an act, too.

"First thing I want to do is see the original," he said to McKenzie.

"You think the owner lied about having it? Why would he do that?" she asked as the house came into view.

"I don't know. To collect on the insurance, maybe. He could be in on some scam involving the artwork if this artist is that well-known."

McKenzie raised a brow as she parked next to a

white SUV next to the house. "Cowboy art doesn't go for that much. A Taylor West might sell for near a hundred grand to the right market. But we aren't talking the Mona Lisa."

He didn't know what the original was worth, but he was anxious to see it. "I looked up the artist's website last night. Most of Taylor West's original work sells for twenty-five to seventy-five thousand depending on the size. Some of his older works are worth more."

"Did you see this particular painting on the artist's website?"

"No."

The owner, Theo Nelson, turned out to be an older distinguished man who'd apparently made his money in real estate back East. "If you have any questions, just let me know. I'll be in my study." Nelson disappeared up the stairs, leaving them alone.

"So what do you think, so far?" McKenzie asked as they stepped to the bank of windows that looked out on Lone Mountain. The snow-covered peak glowed in the morning sun against a robin's-egg-blue sky.

"The view is incredible," Laramie said. Then he dragged his gaze away to look at the paintings on the walls.

"This open concept is nice," McKenzie said as she went into the kitchen. "Great for entertaining. Granite countertops, new top-of-the-line appliances, lots of cupboard space, a walk-in pantry and even more storage for multiple sets of china and glassware—if you ever get married to a woman who collects both... You aren't listening to me," she said when Laramie didn't take the bait.

"Sorry. Let's see the second story," he said, already starting up the stairs.

The next floor had a large second living area, two bedrooms and a study. The study door was partially open, the owner at his desk, head down.

Laramie scanned the walls quickly. The painting wasn't there.

"Another great view," McKenzie was saying.

He agreed, taking a moment to notice the house. He liked it. "Let's see the top floor." He saw her shake her head, but she followed him up to the third level.

This, he realized, was a huge master bedroom. It cantilevered out so when he stood at the bank of windows, he felt as if he was flying.

"Impressive," McKenzie said. "But I'm not sure I could sleep in here. I have this thing about heights. The master bathroom is really nice, though. Check out this shower." She turned, no doubt realizing she'd lost him again.

Laramie stood in front of a painting, shaking his head. "This is the one."

"Does it look like the painting you took from the woman last night?" McKenzie asked in a whisper as she stepped closer.

"It looks *exactly* like it. How can he be so sure it's the original?"

"Because I had it authenticated." Neither of them had heard the owner come up the stairs to join them. Now the man stepped past them to take the painting off the wall and show them the back.

Laramie could see that it had a small card taped to the back. He realized how easy it would have been for the cat burglar to make the switch—including the authertication.

"You must be the man who thought you saw a burglar here last night," Nelson said as he put the painting back on the wall. "I'm glad it was a false alarm."

"Me, too," Laramie said, still not sure he believed it.

"So what do you think of the house?" the man asked.

"I like it."

"We'll be looking at some others," McKenzie said quickly. "How long are you going to be in town?"

"Only as long as it takes. So if you're interested…"

"You'll hear from us," she said, motioning to Laramie that it was time to go. "I have several other houses for us to look at this morning," she said once they were in the SUV heading off the mountain.

"Don't bother. I want that one."

She shot him a look. "But you haven't even—"

"That's the house. Find out what furniture stays. Also I want that painting."

As they dropped over the rise, the house disappearing behind them, McKenzie hit her brakes and skidded to a stop in the middle of the narrow snow-packed road. "You want the painting?"

"I'm pretty sure he'll part with it. If he's selling the house, then he's leaving Montana. His next wife won't want any cowboy art in her house."

McKenzie laughed. "You are definitely decisive once you make up your mind, but did you even look at the house or do you really just want the painting?"

He smiled over at her. "I want both. See what kind of deal you can get me, but don't take no for an answer."

She laughed and shook her head as she got the SUV

going again. "You're more like your brothers than I thought you were."

She had no idea. "I think you're right," Laramie said. "It wasn't my brothers who put that woman up to that stunt last night."

"I'm relieved to hear you say that," she said.

"I think she really *is* a cat burglar."

McKenzie shot him a look. "But she didn't steal anything."

He rubbed his jaw, surprised that he'd forgotten to shave. He'd been so anxious to confront Tag this morning. "I'm not sure about that."

"Why am I getting a bad feeling that you're thinking of trying to catch this woman?"

He smiled over at her. He knew he could go to his brothers for help. Hayes was a private investigator and Austin, who'd been a deputy sheriff, now worked for Hayes at his investigative business.

But his cat burglar had made this personal. He wanted to catch her himself.

Chapter Three

"I know Taylor West's work well," the art dealer said when Laramie called. "Who did you say gave you my name?"

"Local Realtor McKenzie Sheldon Cardwell. She said she's worked with you before."

"Oh, yes, McKenzie," Herbert Darlington said. "You have a painting you'd like me to authenticate?"

"If you can."

Darlington made an unpleasant sound. "If it is a true Taylor West work, I will be able to tell at once. When would you like me to take a look at it?"

"I'm parked outside your gallery right now."

The gallery was in a narrow building along the main street of Bozeman. Laramie had driven the forty-five miles first thing that morning. He was anxious to know about the painting. Even more anxious to know about the woman who'd gotten away.

Golden light shone on the paintings on the old brick walls of the gallery as he entered. He looked for any by Taylor West and saw several of Native Americans as well as one of cowboys. This one, though, was a cattle drive filled with longhorns and cowboys driving the herd through a canyon. It looked so real he could almost smell the dust the cattle were kicking up.

"Bring it back here," Darlington said motioning to a door at the back. The man was short and thick with thinning hair above a round red face. He wore a dark suit like an undertaker and sported a narrow black mustache above narrow thin lips.

Without another word, Darlington took the framed painting from him and moved over to a table. He snapped on a light, pulled on a pair of glasses and bent over the artwork.

"Where did you get this?" he asked after a moment.

"I picked it up from an unknown source."

Darlington shot him a look over one shoulder before returning to the painting. "It's quite good."

"But it's not a Taylor West."

"I didn't say that."

Laramie waited impatiently as the man pulled out a magnifying glass and went over the entire painting again. So much for being able to tell at a glance.

After a few minutes, Darlington let out a sigh, took off his glasses, snapped off the light and turned. "It's an original Taylor West."

Laramie let out a laugh as he raked a hand through his hair. How was that possible? How did any of this make sense? It didn't. "You're sure?"

The art expert gave him a pained, insulted look. "I'm guessing you picked it up for a song."

"Something like that." He reached for the painting.

"So you're interested in selling it," Darlington said. "I suppose I could make you an offer."

"It's not for sale." He reached again for the painting and this time the gallery owner handed it over, though reluctantly.

"I would be happy to authenticate it for you in writing," the gallery owner said.

Laramie wondered if he'd authenticated the one now hanging in the house he hoped McKenzie was getting for him. "I'll think about it." The art dealer walked him toward the front door.

Just then a tall, thin older man with a shoulder-length mane of white-blond hair and a handlebar mustache came in on a gust of wind. He looked like something out of an Old West movie.

"Cody can verify what I've told you," Darlington said.

Laramie eyed the man, wondering if he was also considered an art expert.

"Cody Kent is another of our Western artists," the gallery owner said. Then he turned to Cody. "Mr. Cardwell brought in a Taylor West painting. He was questioning its authenticity."

"Really?" Cody tilted his head to look at the painting in Laramie's hand as Darlington explained to him that while this was a one-of-a-kind piece, apparently there was another one owned by another collector.

That definitely got the man's attention. "So you're saying one of them is a forgery?"

"I'd stake my reputation that this is the original," Darlington said, puffing himself up. "Do you agree?"

Laramie handed the man the artwork and watched him as he inspected it. He noticed that the man's hands seemed to tremble as he stared at it.

The artist handed it back. "Sure looks like the real

thing to me." Cody Kent's gaze met his. "Where did you get it?"

"Just picked it up recently," Laramie said. He took it back from the older man. "Glad to hear you both agree it is an authentic Taylor West."

As he headed for the door, Darlington followed. "Well, if you decide to get rid of it…"

Laramie shook his head but then stopped just short of the door to ask, "How much would you say it's worth?" He noticed that Cody Kent had moved to one of the paintings on display only yards from them, clearly listening to the conversation.

Darlington seemed to give a price more thought than was necessary since he'd just offered to buy it. "I could give you…thirty," he said, keeping his voice down.

"Thirty?"

"Thirty *thousand*," Darlington said. "It would be more but it's an older piece. His work has improved over the years."

Was that right? Laramie smiled to himself. From what he'd seen online last night, artists' older work appeared to have more value—especially if the artist was now dead. Taylor West was still kicking, apparently, but Laramie suspected the painting must be worth a lot more that what he was being offered.

"Thanks, but I think I'll keep it," he said as he tucked it under his arm. "It has…sentimental value."

SID PUT ON clean jeans and a sweater to go to the grocery store. Often she went in her paint-streaked pants and shirts. Anyone who paid any attention was aware that she painted since she spent most Saturdays at the local craft show selling her wares.

Not her paintings, but haphazardly done Montana scenes on everything from old metal saw blades and antique milk cans to ancient tractor parts and windmill blades. Amazingly, her crafts sold well, which proved to her that most people didn't know the difference between good art and bad.

But today she wanted to fly under the radar. No reason to call attention to herself as an artist. It might be too risky if the man from last night was still in town. She knew she was being silly. He'd probably completely forgotten about her.

She assumed he would have gone to the marshal last night with a story about her robbing that house. Since the painting wouldn't be missing, she wasn't worried.

Her only regret was losing the painting. She needed it. Which meant she had to get it back. Or taking all these chances would have been for nothing.

Where was the painting now? She'd learned at a young age to make friends where needed. Now she picked up the phone and called her friend who worked at the marshal's office as she drove to the grocery store.

After the usual pleasantries, she said, "So what's new down there?" Dispatcher Tara Kirkwood loved her job because she got to know everything that was going on—and she loved to share it.

"Counterfeit bills keep turning up," Tara said, keeping her voice down although the office was small and she was probably the only person down there right then. The marshal and detectives were probably out.

She and Tara had established long ago that anything Tara told her wouldn't go any further—and it never had. "The marshal is chasing one right now that was passed at the Corral Bar."

"No more cat burglar sightings?" she asked after listening to what Tara knew about the counterfeit bills.

"Actually, before Hud left, he said his wife's cousin who is in town caught the cat burglar last night." She laughed. "According to him, the burglar turned out to be a *her.*"

"No kidding? So is she locked up down there?"

"Naw, she got away." Tara laughed again. "Hud got a chuckle out of it since apparently there was no crime and his cousin-in-law was quite taken with the woman."

Sid laughed even though this was not what she wanted to hear. The marshal's cousin-in-law? Just her luck. Not to mention "quite taken with her"? *Really?* She thought of the kiss. It might have been a mistake since she'd had a hard time forgetting about it, as well.

"What's the guy's name?" she asked.

"Laramie Cardwell."

Cardwell? Anyone who lived in the Gallatin Canyon knew that name. The Cardwell Ranch was one of the first established in the canyon. But she'd never heard of a Laramie Cardwell before.

"You said he was in town. So he's not from here?" she asked even though she knew his accent was way too Southern.

"His father is Angus Cardwell. Apparently his mother got a divorce years ago and took her five sons to live in Texas. Laramie's up here from Houston. He and his brothers own that new place, Texas Boys Barbecue."

"Huh."

"Have you tried it yet?" Tara asked.

"No. I've been meaning to, though," she said, realizing it was true.

"It's really good."

"So did the so-called cat burglar get away with anything?" she had to ask. "You said no crime was committed?"

"Laramie found a painting, but it wasn't stolen from the house. I overheard Hud say Laramie is hanging on to it. Kind of like a souvenir."

Sid mouthed a silent oath. She'd reached Meadow Village and the grocery store. "So now it's hanging at Cardwell Ranch," she joked.

"More than likely at his new house," Tara said.

"His new house?"

The dispatcher dropped her voice even further. "The house that he caught her allegedly robbing? He's *buying* it."

Sid pulled into a parking spot in front of the store. Tara was always a wealth of information. "Now that is a coincidence," she said. "So apparently he's staying."

"At least for the holidays I would think. You really should try their barbecue. It is *so* good."

"I just might do that. Got to go. Sure hope they catch those counterfeiters."

"Me, too. Hud is fit to be tied. It will be nice when things die back down around here."

Disconnecting, Sid parked in front of the grocery, thinking about everything Tara had said. How was she going to get the painting back? She'd never been one to push her luck and hitting the same house twice was more than risky, especially since now Laramie

Cardwell might be expecting her. But did she really have a choice?

Her stomach growled. Still hungry and realizing it was almost lunchtime, she looked up the hill at the sign for Texas Boys Barbecue.

THE FAMILY HAD gathered at the Cardwell Ranch for lunch. Everyone but Laramie.

"What's going on with him?" Austin asked. For years he had been the no-show brother, the one who caught grief because he didn't play family well. Since meeting Gillian and returning to his birthplace, he'd changed. He loved these family get-togethers.

"He's looking for the cat burglar," McKenzie said. "And the four of you can blame yourself for that if you're behind this."

"What?" Austin asked, looking around the table. Tag told him what he knew, Hud added his part and McKenzie finished it up. *"Seriously?* Laramie is trying to find this woman?" He turned to Tag. "You told him we had nothing to do with this, right?"

"I swore we didn't."

Austin groaned. "So he might actually be chasing a real cat burglar."

"Only if the cat burglar is a young woman with silvery-blue eyes," Hud said, shaking his head. "This whole cat burglar thing started when a few residents saw a dark-clad figure sneaking around a couple of houses. But the bottom line is that no one has reported being burglarized. No valuables or paintings are missing."

"So you think it's a hoax," Austin said.

"I do," the marshal agreed. "Probably the local security company put the woman up to it to drum up more business. A lot of the people in Big Sky are from urban areas so security is a concern for them. The rest of us locals don't even bother to lock our doors."

"He told me he was going to visit the artist whose painting the woman dropped," McKenzie said between bites. "Taylor West. He lives up the canyon near Taylor Fork."

"Why didn't he come to us?" Austin asked his brother Hayes. "We are actually trained for this sort of thing." He'd gone to work for Hayes's detective agency after quitting the sheriff's department in Texas—he hadn't been satisfied being simply retired. Gillian had been right. He'd been miserable. He was too young to retire and he enjoyed investigative work.

"Seriously?" Dana asked. "You don't understand why your brother might want to solve this thing on his own? It involves an apparently attractive woman who tricked him and escaped. Laramie is related to all of you. Enough said. He probably thinks she's in trouble and is off to save her."

They all laughed, but Austin couldn't shake the bad feeling he had.

"I know that look in your eye," Gillian said to Austin. "Don't do it."

"She's right," Jackson said speaking up. "We need to stay out of this. I think Laramie's been getting bored running the business. Why not let him have a little... fun, since there is nothing to the cat burglar stories?"

They all agreed. Except Austin. "*Fun?* What if this woman is dangerous?"

"Laramie can take care of himself," Hayes said. "He hasn't just been sitting behind a desk for the past ten years. He's worked with some of us on cases. I think Jackson's right. He needs this and he needs us to stay out of it."

Austin couldn't help being protective of his youngest brother. While he and Hayes had both worked in law enforcement, Laramie had no experience dealing with criminals.

"I hope you're right," Austin said as he watched his family finish their lunches. Still, he couldn't shake the feeling that Laramie had no idea what he was getting into.

For the time being, he'd stay out of it since, if Hud was right, it had been nothing but a prank. But if a woman was involved…

Chapter Four

Artist Taylor West was a tall drink of water. At least that's how Laramie had seen him described on his website. The man who opened the door at the West home *was* tall. He'd aged, though, since he'd put his photo on his website. Laramie guessed he must be in his sixties and had once been very handsome. The gray hair at his temples gave him a distinguished look, but his complexion told the story of a man who drank too much.

"I don't usually meet clients at my home," West said, looking put out.

Laramie was glad he hadn't called ahead. "This was a matter that couldn't wait." A photograph on the wall behind the man caught Laramie's attention. It was of Taylor with a pretty young green-eyed blonde. He was staring at the photo more intently than he realized— especially at the eyes. Could this be the woman he'd tackled last night? She looked the right size but the eye color was wrong.

"My wife, Jade," West said.

Laramie blinked in surprise. Given the age difference between the artist and the woman in the photo, he would have thought it was West's daughter.

West's gaze went to the painting Laramie was holding in one hand. "Is that one of mine?" He sounded like a man worried that Laramie had come here to complain.

"That's what I'd like to know. I promise not to take any more of your time than necessary."

"What makes you think it's mine?" West asked.

"Because it has your name on it." He didn't mention that the so-called expert at the gallery had authenticated it.

"Well, fine, come on in out of the cold. This shouldn't take long." He didn't look less perturbed, but he did step back to let Laramie in.

But that was as far as the invitation was extended. Standing in the entryway of the house, Laramie uncovered the painting and handed it to the artist. Past West, he could see that the house was a huge mess. So where was the young wife?

West looked at it and said, "I don't see what the problem is," and started to hand it back.

"So it's yours?" Laramie asked.

"Obviously," the artist said with impatience.

"Then there *is* a problem." He told him about the one that Theo Nelson owned, the one that had been authenticated. "How do you explain that?"

"One of them must be a forgery since I only painted one."

"And you're sure this one is the original?"

West snatched the painting from him and with a curse headed down a hallway. Laramie followed, stepping over boots and shoes, jackets, dirty socks and assorted dog toys.

"The cleaning crew comes tomorrow," West said

over his shoulder before turning into what was obviously his studio. It, too, was in disarray.

Laramie suspected the man didn't have anyone to clean the house. Or the young wife to do so, either, for that matter.

West snapped on a lamp and put the painting under it. "Where did you get this?"

"I picked it up recently."

"Nelson is right. If he has the original, then this one isn't mine," West said.

"Are you sure?" Clearly he wasn't. "I should tell you that before I came here, I took the painting to a local expert," Laramie said. "He confirmed it was yours and offered me thirty thousand for it."

The artist's eyes widened in surprise. "The original is worth over fifty."

Just as Laramie had suspected. "But the question is, which is the original?"

West swore. "If this is a forgery, it's a really good one." The man was frowning at the artwork, clearly angry and also seeming confused.

"I've looked at both. They appear identical. So if you didn't paint the copy, then who did?"

The artist shook his head. "How would I know?" He was upset now.

"It would take some talent, wouldn't it?"

West sighed impatiently. "Sure, but—"

"Otherwise, you're saying any art student could copy your paintings?"

"I see what you're getting at," the older man said angrily. "Yes, it takes talent. A *lot* of talent. They would have had to have studied their craft and have some natural ability, as well. Also they would have had to study my work. Not just anyone could make a reproduction this good."

"So has this person been hiding under a rock, or is it someone you know?"

West seemed shocked by the question. "It couldn't possibly be anyone I know."

"Why not? I would think the cowboy art market is very small. It must also be competitive. There can't be that many of you painting at this level, right?"

The artist nodded. "There are only twenty of us in the OWAC." Seeing Laramie's quizzical expression, he elaborated. "The Old West Artists Coalition."

Laramie considered that. "Only twenty? That sounds like a pretty elite—and competitive—group."

"We're all *friends*. We encourage and support each other. The only competition is with ourselves to get better."

"But some of you must make more money than others," he prodded. "Who is the best paid of this group of cowboy artists?"

West met his gaze with an arrogant one. "I am, but there are several others who do quite well."

"And you're telling me there is no jealousy?" Laramie scoffed at that. He knew too well, being one of five brothers, that competition was in male DNA. "So who are the others who are doing 'quite well'?"

"Cody Kent and Hank Ramsey, in that order. Rock Jackson quite a ways behind those two."

Laramie couldn't help but laugh. Just the fact that West knew that proved *he* at least had a competitive spirit. "So what exactly does this group do?"

"I told you. We support each other. We came together because of a desire to keep this art form alive in memory of the greats like the late Frederic Remington and Charles M. Russell. But also to ensure the work is an authentic representation of Western life. Without standards of quality and a respect for each other and the work..." He sounded as if he was quoting the group's bylaws.

"And you belong to this group?"

"I'm one of its founders along with Rock, Hank and Cody Kent," he said proudly.

Laramie had heard something in the man's tone. "What does it take to be a member?"

"You have to apply. The members decide if your work and your character meet our standards."

"Your *standards*?"

"Originally, you had to have cowboy experience as well as talent. That's changed some. Why are you asking me all this?" West demanded.

Laramie wasn't sure. "So it's an exclusive...club."

"None of my fellow artists would have any reason to rip me off by duplicating my work, if that's what you're getting at," West said. "Not to mention, most of them don't have the talent to copy my work."

Laramie tried not to smile. No competition here.

"Look," West said as if he knew he'd said too much. "There aren't that many of us. We're a dying breed of artists who care about our work. The satisfaction comes from painting and selling our own work—not copying someone else's and passing it off for money."

"Even if they needed money badly?" Laramie asked.

He saw something change in West's expression as if the question had made him think of someone. Laramie knew money could be the most obvious reason for making forgeries of Taylor West's work. Or maybe to rub West's arrogant face in it.

West picked up the painting, frowning harder as he studied it again. "This is definitely the original," he said, but he seemed to lack conviction.

"If no one in your group is talented enough to make you question if this painting is yours or not…"

"I'm telling you," West snapped, "there's no one alive who could have copied my work well enough to fool an expert, let alone me."

Laramie thought that was a ridiculous statement given that someone obviously had, and he said as much.

West suddenly looked even more upset. "There is one man," the artist said after a moment. He'd paled. "H. F. Powell."

"Where would I find him?"

West didn't seem to hear him for a moment. He shook his head as if clearing away cobwebs from his brain. "Find him?" His laugh was more of a grunt. "Six feet under, last I checked."

TEXAS? SO THAT was Laramie Cardwell's accent, Sid thought. The barbecue restaurant had opened in Big Sky Meadows just last year. She'd heard it was owned by five brothers from Houston. Since she didn't get out much—at least during the day—that had been all Sid knew about the place.

Good sense told her to go into the store, buy some food and take it back to the cabin. The sooner she got home, the sooner she could get ready for tonight. Last night's close call was a good reminder that she needed to finish this and move on.

But barbecue sounded good. More than anything, she was curious. She quickly shopped for what groceries she needed, telling herself she would get a barbecue sandwich to go. She knew she was taking a risk, but then again, she'd been taking risks for some time now. Putting the groceries into the back of her SUV, she walked quickly up the hill to Texas Boys Barbecue on the recently plowed sidewalk. The sun glistening off the snow was almost blinding. It was one of those clear, cold winter days in Big Sky when she could see her breath as she walked. She looked up at Lone Mountain, momentarily stunned by how beautiful it was this morning.

Sometimes she got so busy she forgot to notice what an amazing place this was. Once she was done with all of this, maybe she would take a few weeks off and snowboard up on the mountain. She deserved it after this.

A bell jangled over the door as she entered the restaurant. It was early so the place was busy but not packed, and there were enough people that she didn't think she would stand out. Not that she believed Laramie Cardwell could recognize her.

The aroma of smoked meat filled the air, making her stomach growl again. Slipping into a booth, she pulled out a menu from behind an array of barbecue sauces with names like Hot in Houston and Sweet and Spicy San Antonio.

She'd just opened it when she heard a male voice with a distinct Southern accent coming from the kitchen. Looking up she saw a head of dark hair. The man was talking to another man with the same accent. As the first man turned, she realized he wasn't the one from last night, but the resemblance gave her a start even before she laid eyes on the second man.

It was him!

Suddenly, as if sensing her staring at him, he glanced in her direction. Sid quickly ducked behind her menu as a young waitress approached her booth.

"What can I get you?" asked a teenaged girl with a ponytail and an order pad.

"I'll try the pulled pork sandwich with beans and coleslaw," Sid said from behind her menu. "Can I get that to go?"

"Great choice. What would you like to drink?" the girl asked.

Sid peeked out from behind the menu. Through the window into the kitchen she could no longer see the two men—nor could she hear them. Maybe they'd left.

"And a beer."

The girl nodded, then shyly asked if she could see her ID. "I'm sorry, but I have to ask."

Sid might have found that amusing since she was thirty. But she was aware that she didn't look a day over twenty. Behind the waitress, she heard the men's voices coming from the kitchen again. They sounded as though they were arguing.

She heard one say he didn't like what the other one was doing. "Austin, if I need your help I'll ask for it. I can handle this." Laramie Cardwell's voice. Handle what?

Sid looked up at the waitress. Today of all days, she didn't want to show her ID. She knew it was silly since Laramie Cardwell hadn't seen her face last night. But he might have a few moments ago. She remembered him above her in the moonlight and the way he'd looked into her eyes…and felt a shiver.

"You know, just make it a cola. I have work to do this afternoon."

The poor girl nodded without looking at her and wrote on her order pad.

"The owners of this place, are they really from Texas?" Sid asked.

The girl brightened. "They sure are. Five brothers. They just opened this place, but I heard there's another one going to open at Red Lodge."

"Really? Five brothers, huh?"

"Yep, all raised in Texas. They were born here, but left when they were kids. Four of them have moved back."

"The fifth one?" Sid asked, remembering how strong the man's Texas accent had been.

"Laramie still lives in Houston. That's where the main office is located. He's the one in charge of all the restaurants. They're cousins to Dana Cardwell of Cardwell Ranch, if you're familiar with the area."

Anyone who lived in the Canyon as the Gallatin Canyon was known had heard of the Cardwells of Cardwell Ranch.

"Their story is on the back of the menu, if you're interested. I'll get your order right out," the girl said. "You want that cola while you wait?"

Sid would much rather have had a beer and felt foolish for not showing the girl her ID. What were the chances that the waitress would remember her name or have any reason to mention it to her bosses?

Glancing toward the kitchen, she didn't see the men. Or hear them, but that didn't mean they weren't still back there. And if the man from last night had seen her a few minutes ago…

"Sure, I'll take the cola now, but make it to go," she said as she picked up the menu and turned it over.

The Cardwell brothers' story was on the back along with their photos. What surprised her was that Texas Boys Barbecue was a franchise the brothers had started. She'd just assumed they only owned this one restaurant.

Less surprising was that all five brothers were drop-dead gorgeous. In the photo on the back of the menu, the photographer had lined them up along a jack-legged fence, a ranch house in the background. Each brother wore jeans, boots, Western shirts and Stetsons. Each was equally handsome.

Her gaze went to Laramie. He was definitely the one who'd tackled her last night. She felt a shiver as she looked at his photo. His blue eyes stared back at her almost challenging. She told herself she had nothing to fear. He didn't know who she was or the marshal would have been to her door already. Even if he had bought that house, he'd be like most of the residents—staying only a few weeks of the year.

She wished she could wait for him to return to Texas. Unfortunately, she couldn't. Time was running out. She had to get the painting back—even knowing there was a chance of crossing paths with Laramie Cardwell again. She would just have to make sure that didn't happen.

Chapter Five

Laramie left the restaurant, his mind on the painting and the woman, of course. The winter day sparkled under a blinding sun that ricocheted off the new-fallen snow. At loose ends waiting to hear if McKenzie got him the house, he went for a drive up the canyon.

Next to the highway, the Gallatin River snaked through the canyon under a thick layer of aquamarine ice. He tried to enjoy the beauty of this alien winter place. The snowcapped pines bent under the weight of their frozen burden, reminding him that it was less than a week until Christmas. His cousin Dana loved the holidays and went all-out surrounded by her family. He smiled at the thought.

Glancing in his review mirror, he realized he'd seen the large dark brown older-model sedan behind him before—right after he'd left Taylor West's house. It was behind him again.

He tried to laugh off the thought of someone following him. First cat burglars now this? Well, there was one way to find out, he thought as he neared the Corral Bar. He slowed and pulled in. The car went on past.

The windows on the vehicle had been tinted, so he hadn't gotten a good look at the driver. If he had to guess, he'd say male. As it disappeared up the road, he told himself the driver hadn't been following him anyway.

He thought about going inside the bar and having a burger and a beer. This was his father and uncle's favorite bar. Their band often played here.

But he was too antsy. He wanted to get back and find out if McKenzie had gotten him the house…and the painting. He pulled back on the road headed toward Big Sky again, his thoughts going to his cat burglar. The forgery at the house had to have been painted by someone with a whole lot of talent as Taylor West had said.

So if it was a forgery, who had painted it? Not some dead man named H. F. Powell unless he'd painted it before his demise. But the big question was why would his thief take it instead of the authenticated original?

She wouldn't. So if he was right and she'd been coming out of the house when he'd arrived, then she'd been in the process of stealing the original when he'd stopped her.

Which meant McKenzie was about to make a deal for a forgery.

Shaking his head at his own foolishness, he glanced in his rearview mirror. The brown car was back.

He felt a start at the sight of it behind him again. As he glanced in his rearview mirror again he saw that the vehicle was coming up fast. The canyon road had been plowed, but the dark pavement was still icy. Add to that the twists and turns the highway took as it wound through the Gallatin Canyon and the driver of the car was going way too fast.

Laramie had only a moment for his brain to take it

all in before he realized that the driver had no intention of slowing down. A curve was coming up, one with a steep rock face on one side of the road and a precarious drop to the frozen river on the other.

He felt the vehicle's bumper connect with the back of his rental. Just a tap. But on the icy road that was all it took. The rental SUV began to fishtail on the ice as the dark car bumped into him again. He could feel the tires lose traction and the next thing he knew he was sliding toward the river. He felt the tires go off the pavement. A wall of snow rushed over the hood.

Expecting the SUV would be pitched into the river and break through the ice, Laramie braced him. Moments later, heart in his throat, he was shocked when the deep snow off the side of the highway stopped his descent just yards from the frozen river. He sat, so shaken he didn't notice the dark car backing up on the highway above him until he heard the roar of the engine.

Looking up, all he saw was the dark tinted windows on the passenger side as the car sped away.

THE PULLED PORK sandwich was to die for, just as Tara had said. Sid couldn't believe she hadn't been to Texas Boys Barbecue before this. The beans and coleslaw were quite good, too. She had downed the cola on the drive back to the cabin but had saved the rest until she'd reached home. Once there, she'd pulled a cold bottle of beer from the grocery bag and sat down at her kitchen table to devour the barbecue. She couldn't help licking her fingers.

Her father would have loved the food, she thought, and then pushed the thought away. While he was always with her, driving her more than ambition, remembering him often brought aching pain. One day that pain would go away, once she accomplished the job she'd set for herself, she told herself as she cleaned up the mess and changed her clothes.

Back at her easel, she considered the painting she was working on. It was one of her father. He was standing by a horse next to the corral. His battered straw cowboy hat was pushed back, sunlight on his weathered face. Behind him were the rocky cliffs and scrub pine of her youth. She was painting it from memory since all the photos had been lost.

She thought of the stash of original artwork she had hidden all these years. It had been years since anyone had seen those paintings—herself included.

Until recently.

LARAMIE CALLED 911 the moment he was out of the SUV and standing at the edge of the highway. He couldn't believe how lucky he'd been. Just a few more yards and the rental would have been in the river.

Marshal Hud Savage came on the line. "What's this about you being forced off the road?"

He told him and Hud promised to have a wrecker sent down to get his rental out of the snowbank.

Laramie had given him what little description he could of the vehicle that had forced him off the road. As with the alleged cat burglar, he had little information other than the car was large and brown with tinted windows.

"It happened too fast," he said. "But there was no doubt of the driver's intent." He could almost see Hud nodding.

"Had you passed the driver? Or had any interaction before this?"

"No. I saw the car earlier up by Taylor Fork, then again later when I went for a drive up the canyon." He could tell that Hud had little hope of finding the vehicle. "Can you do me a favor? Find out what Taylor West drives."

"Taylor West, the local artist?" Hud asked with obvious surprise.

Hud told him that West owned a large SUV and an older-model pickup. Neither matched the description Laramie had given him.

"What makes you think Taylor West had anything to do with running you off the road?" Hud had wanted to know.

"Nothing really," Laramie said. "That's just the first place I noticed the car following me, after I visited the artist. I'm probably wrong about there being a connection." And yet he had a feeling that if Taylor hadn't been behind it, then someone he knew definitely was. But he had no idea why. "Maybe I ticked off the driver somehow."

"Maybe," Hud said. "You sure you weren't going too slow?"

"Maybe."

TAYLOR WEST PACED the floor after the Texan left. He'd been so shaken that he would have poured himself a drink if there'd been any booze in the house. But his wife had dumped every drop she could find down the drain before she'd left. He'd dug out enough from his hiding places that he'd been fine. Until now.

"When are you coming back?" he'd demanded as

he'd watched her throw her clothes into two suitcases and head for the door.

"When you get some help with your drinking."

He didn't need any help. He drank fine without it.

The old joke fell flat. He knew it was more than his drinking. She'd been trying to let him down easy, he thought as he looked around the house. He hadn't realized what a mess it was until he'd seen it through his visitor's eyes. What had Laramie Cardwell been thinking, showing up unannounced at his door like that?

"It's that damned painting," he said as he opened one kitchen cupboard after another, not even sure what he was looking for—then he remembered where he'd hidden a bottle of bourbon months ago and felt better.

In the laundry room, he moved the washer out a little. Reaching behind it, he groped around, feeling nothing but air and cobwebs. Panic filled him. The drive to the nearest liquor store was a good ten miles. He couldn't go to the nearest bar since he'd been kicked out of it.

His hand brushed over the cold throat of the bourbon bottle. His relief rushed out in a laugh that sounded too loud in the small room. Clutching the bottle, he'withdrew it, wiped off the dust with one of his dirty shirts lying on the laundry room floor and headed for the kitchen.

Unable to find a clean glass, he took his first drink straight from the bottle. The liquor bathed his tongue in bliss, warmed his throat and quenched his thirst. He took another drink as the first one reached his belly and sent a golden glow through him.

That's when he knew he was in trouble. There was only one man who could have painted the forgery. He'd be kidding himself if he thought it was anyone but H. F. Powell. He thought of Powell's last words to him. "I could paint one of your pieces and you wouldn't know the difference, that's how good I am."

Taylor shook his head. He hadn't let himself think of H.F. in years. Some things were best forgotten. Everyone knew that the painter had become a recluse in the last years of his life. No one had seen him for almost two years before the tragedy. There hadn't been a funeral—at H.F.'s request. No memorial service. No family.

H.F. must be rolling in his grave since his paintings were now worth a small fortune. Taylor admitted grudgingly, the man had been one hell of a painter. But look where it had gotten him. The arrogant old fool had died alone and miserable.

Just like you're going to die. Taylor snorted at the thought and the one that came after it. *What goes around, comes around.* He shuddered and took another drink, regretting the calls he'd made the moment Laramie Cardwell left. But he'd been so upset and he wasn't in this alone.

Rock Jackson had sounded as if he'd been asleep before the call.

"I'm telling you this painting was so good... I'm not even sure it isn't the original," he'd told Rock. "Tell me there isn't any chance—"

"Take it easy. You're jumping to conclusions. Who brought you the painting?"

Taylor told him.

"The guy's gone, right?"

"He just left."

"Then there is nothing to worry about," Rock had

said. "Look, I have to go. Have a drink. Everything is fine."

Artist Hank Ramsey had told him pretty much the same thing, only Taylor had heard more worry in Hank's voice.

"If you had seen this painting…" Taylor had said feeling sick to his stomach.

Hank had asked the name of the man who'd stopped by and what painting it had been. Hank had tried to calm him back down. "Taylor, we're all painting cowboys, horses and Indians. We've all had someone copy our paintings. Since you're at the top of the heap, your paintings are going to be forged the most. Let me see what I can find out. In the meantime, don't do anything crazy."

He'd hung up, thinking about the other members of OWAC, picturing each of their faces and telling himself that none of them were good enough to paint such a perfect forgery.

He'd tried to call Rock back, but the number had gone to voice mail. "This is Taylor West. Call me. We really need to talk. If that painting is what I think it is… Call me." He'd disconnected, wondering where Rock was. Or if he just wasn't taking his calls after the first one. Which would make Rock look pretty suspicious, wouldn't it?

Now he took a long drink, admitting that he never should have trusted Rock. Rock wasn't that much different from H. F. Powell when it came to women. Now Rock was in trouble because of another woman. In the middle of an ugly divorce, he was probably desperate for money. But how far would he go?

Taylor knew his suspicion of Rock could also be because Rock had always been jealous of him—especially when Taylor had married Jade.

Jade. Where was his beautiful young wife? She'd probably gone to her mother's back in Indiana. He shoved the thought of her away as he took another drink. He had a lot more to worry about than Jade.

"THE HOUSE IS YOURS," McKenzie announced when Laramie stopped by her office after getting his rental SUV pulled out of the snowbank. He was still shaken, but even more determined to get to the bottom of whatever was going on.

"And the painting?" he asked expectantly. He told himself he couldn't be sure which was original and without it, he might never know.

She chuckled. "Yours, as well. He wanted extra for it, but I convinced him that you wanted pretty much everything in the house except, of course, any items that he couldn't possibly part with. If you don't want the furniture, I know a consignment place—"

"No, furnished is perfect. So what is he leaving?"

"Everything, including the kitchen sink, except for the other paintings and sculptures. He has an art dealer coming to take the lot of them this afternoon."

Laramie couldn't hide his relief. He wasn't sure why the painting was so important. But what had happened after he'd left Taylor West's house had him convinced the painting was at the heart of it. He thought about the house—where he'd seen his alleged cat burglar. "How soon can I take occupancy?"

"Right away, I suppose, if you're in that much of a hurry."

He'd been staying with Tag and McKenzie and

didn't want to hurt her feelings. "No hurry, just anxious to get settled."

"I can understand that. Since the house will come completely furnished, there won't be much that you will need. He's leaving bedding, all of which he said is brand-new. Apparently they haven't gotten to use this house much. I take it that his soon-to-be-ex wife didn't like it up here. Too isolated. Since you're paying cash, I can arrange a rental agreement until the sale is final. You should be able to move in this evening. The owner is in a hurry to get out of town."

"Great."

"But this…urgency to get settled, it wouldn't have anything to do with your…cat burglar, would it?"

Laramie smiled to himself. "You sound like Austin. I ran into him earlier at the restaurant. Like I told him, I know what I'm doing." He wished that was true.

But he didn't think the earlier incident was an attempt to kill him. Then what had it been? If the driver had wanted to scare him off, then he'd failed. Laramie was more determined than ever. He was counting on his cat burglar coming back for the painting. It was just a gut feeling, but a strong one, that for some reason she really needed that painting. And he really needed answers.

He stood to leave.

"Don't forget this," McKenzie said reaching behind her. She handed him what Theo Nelson believed to be the original painting.

He stared at it, anxious to compare it to the one in his rented SUV. "Question, if I wanted everyone to know I'd bought the house, how would I go about getting the word out?"

McKenzie laughed. "In a small community like Big Sky? Are you kidding? Everyone knows everyone else's business. It's probably already out there since the owner informed me to go ahead and change the security information to yours. You'll need to change over the utilities and everything else as soon as you get into the house. But if you were to stop by the furniture store or the grocery and happen to mention you'd bought a house…"

"Let me know when you have my key, and thank you so much. Oh, and one more thing. Have you ever heard of an artist by the name of H. F. Powell?"

"Of course. In fact, one of his paintings is coming up for auction at the Christmas ball this year. It's expected to go high. This interest in cowboy art…"

"Just curiosity."

She laughed. "Uh-huh."

Laramie realized how little he knew about art in general as he left for Meadow Village. His plan was to do exactly what McKenzie had suggested. He had a feeling that his cat burglar kept her ear to the ground. How else had she known that the house was supposed to be empty last night?

Chapter Six

Sid rubbed her back. It ached from hours spent painting. She hadn't realized how long she'd been working. When she painted, time flew by. She hadn't even noticed that her back was aching until a few moments ago when she finally laid down her brush.

She also realized she was hungry. Going to the fridge, she peered in. She'd bought the basics at the store, but nothing appealed to her. The pulled pork barbecue sandwich came to mind. Why not go back there? Several good reasons came to her. Except once she thought of barbecue, nothing else would do.

This late in the evening, Texas Boys Barbecue was quiet. Only a few booths were taken. She slipped into one and was thankful when a different waitress came out with a menu.

"We have a special, if you're interested," the young woman said. She rattled off a variety of items, but all Sid keyed in on was the words *ribs*. Her stomach growled.

"I'll take the baby-back rib special." She started to say "to go" but stopped herself. "And a beer." As she started to whip out her ID, she realized the waitress wasn't even going to ask for it. With relief, she put it away, sat back and took in the place in a way she hadn't done earlier. It was nicely done. Comfortable and homey but without kitschy knickknacks. The atmosphere was warm and welcoming and the smells coming out of the kitchen were making her mouth water.

It felt good to be out of her cabin. She sat back, relaxing—until she heard voices in the kitchen as the waitress brought out her beer. Taking a sip, she watched the back, hoping to get another look at Laramie Cardwell. From where she sat, she could hear the conversation. This time there were three men, all of them speaking with a Texas drawl. But no Laramie.

"So he got the house?"

"He's moving in tonight."

"What was the rush?"

"Apparently he's anxious to get settled."

"I hope that's all it is."

"Bet Dana is already planning a housewarming."

Laughter before the three left.

Laramie was moving into the house *tonight*?

So Tara's information had been right, not that she'd doubted it. Sid thought about Laramie showing up so late the night before at the Nelson house on the side of the mountain. He'd only been interested in the house, but he'd stumbled onto her. Just her luck.

"I'm sorry," Sid said getting the waitress's attention. "But could I have that order to go?"

LARAMIE WAS AT the grocery store when McKenzie called to say she had the key to the house. "Do you want to meet at the house?"

"Sounds great. I'm picking up a few things. I can meet you there in thirty minutes."

He quickly got what he needed and headed for the checkout. In a matter of minutes he would have the key to his house. He owned a high-rise condo in Houston, but he had never been this excited about the purchase even though the condo had an amazing view of the city.

The house was perfect for him since he didn't plan to spend that much time in Montana. But he needed his own place when he did. If anything, he thought he might spend more time here—during the summer months.

Would he love the house as much if his cat burglar didn't come back for the painting? He pushed that thought away, telling himself he was in the market for a house long before he'd laid eyes on the dark-clad figure running along the rooftop. Long before the kiss.

At the checkout, he was impatient to get into the house. He had to wait in line behind a half dozen people and wished now that he hadn't bothered. Glancing around, he studied the other people in the line. The tourists were easy to spot in the latest ski gear or after-ski wear.

Out of the corner of his eye, he noticed a bulletin board. Dana had mentioned that there were always people looking for housecleaning jobs around Big Sky, if he needed help.

A poster with cowboy art on it caught his eye. A name jumped out at him. H. F. Powell. Leaving his basket to save his place in line, Laramie quickly stepped to the board. Western Art Exhibit at the Museum of the Rockies in Bozeman. H. F. Powell was one of the artists featured in what the poster said was a rare exhibit of the Western masters.

Hurriedly, he searched the poster for the date, fearing he had missed the exhibit. With relief, he saw that it opened tomorrow. Until today, he'd never heard of H. F. Powell. Now he was curious about the man and his work given that Taylor West swore he was the only man who could have duplicated his work so perfectly.

His cat burglar had certainly piqued his interest in Old West art, he thought. After he checked out, he put his groceries in his SUV and walked up the hill to the restaurant for his dinner. The special tonight at Texas Boys Barbecue was ribs so the cook had saved him a slab along with sides.

As he entered the back door, he breathed in the smell of the food, still amazed that his and his brothers' love for barbecue had led to their Texas Boys Barbecue success. None of them ever had to work another day in their lives, but of course they all did have some job because that was the way they were raised. As promised, the cook had his dinner wrapped and ready to take home to his new house.

It was on his way out that he saw a woman as she came out of the front of the restaurant and climbed into a blue SUV.

The woman caught his eye because of the way she moved. No wasted motion, her steps so fluid—and familiar—as she hurried toward her vehicle. He stood there watching her get into the SUV, feeling like a man who'd just seen a ghost.

A thick, long curly mane of strawberry blond hair hung around her shoulders, catching the last of the day's light and making it shine like copper. He held his breath as he watched her slide behind the wheel. The engine revved. She seemed to be in a hurry to get somewhere. Just like that night.

It was her.

All common sense told him that he couldn't possibly have recognized her simply by the way that she moved. There must be dozens of slim young women like her in the area. And yet...

He looked down the hillside to where he'd left his vehicle as she backed up and sped off up the road toward the mountain. There was no way he could reach his vehicle in time. All he could do was watch her get away.

Which was good, he realized. His first impulse had been to go after her. And then what? If only he had been close enough to see her eyes. And those lips. He told himself that if he saw those again, he'd know for certain.

He was thankful he hadn't gone after her and made a fool of himself. He could just imagine what his four brothers would say if he shared this "sighting" with them.

"You need a woman," Tag would say. "Stalking is illegal," Hayes would warn him. "Get a grip," Austin would say. "I agree with Tag. You need a woman bad," Jackson would add.

As the blue SUV disappeared over a rise, he thought they would have been right. What was going on with him? This wasn't like him. He always thought things out before he reacted. And yet last night, he'd gone after what he believed to be a thief without any thought to the risk.

And now he'd almost chased that woman down, and

yet what were the chances she was the same woman? Big Sky wasn't a large community. If McKenzie was right, then the woman might already know who he was. If that had been her... Would she dare go to Texas Boys Barbecue if she knew who he was, though?

He thought of the woman, of those silver-blue eyes, of those bee-stung lips, thought of how she'd tricked him and gotten away. Yes, she would go to the restaurant he and his brothers owned. The woman was a risk taker.

That thought sent a current of excitement through him.

What if she had gone there looking for *him* because she needed to get her hands on the painting—just as he'd suspected?

Laramie went back inside Texas Boys Barbecue. It only took a minute to find the young waitress who'd served the woman. "She didn't happen to use a check or credit card to pay for her dinner, did she?" he asked, crossing his fingers.

"Cash."

He couldn't hide his disappointment.

"Is there a problem?" the waitress asked.

"No, I was just hoping to get her name."

The teen laughed. "All you had to do was ask. I *know* her. That is I've seen her at the craft shows. Her name is Obsidian Forester, but she goes by Sid for short."

"Obsidian." He nodded, silently cheered. He had her name. "Wait, you said craft shows?"

"Yeah, she's one of the exhibitors like me. I make candles and sell them. It's just something I like to do in my spare time since I like crafting."

"What does...Sid sell?"

"She paints scenes on stuff like handsaws, milk jugs, anything that is kind of old and rusted."

He couldn't help the thrill that moved through him. Maybe that really had been her. "So she's an artist," he said more to himself.

"I think she's wasting her talent painting on old junk." The teen shrugged. "But what do I know? People seem to like what she does. She sells more of those paintings than I do candles."

"You don't happen to know where she lives, do you?"

As SID DROVE HOME, she told herself not to let the Texas cowboy rush her. But she could feel the clock ticking. Any good thief knew not to play against the odds. She'd been lucky, but lately she'd been seen. Then last night, almost caught.

Once at the cabin, she ate her ribs. It was already dark. This time of year in the canyon it was pitch-black by five. The ribs were as good or even better than the pulled pork. She licked her fingers after finishing the last one, then cleaned up the kitchen and herself before dressing in all black. Picking up the black ski mask, she headed for her snowmobile.

The next house on her list wasn't far from her cabin, but she took the long way. The owners were spending the holidays in Hawaii. At least that was the intel she'd gotten on them. It would be easy to find out if it was true. The couple drove a huge ivory SUV and left it in the drive when they were there.

For months, she'd done endless research on the houses she planned to hit and the people who owned them. This one was owned by an older couple. He'd been a pilot, she a homemaker. The house was modest by Big Sky standards.

Sid had met both of them at the local art shows. She often struck up conversations, especially with people who had a piece of art she was interested in. Art lovers were quick to talk about the artists they liked. It hadn't been easy to find the owners of the pieces she still needed, but she'd finally tracked them all down.

As she came over a rise, she saw the house. It loomed up out of the darkness. No lights on inside. No large SUV in the drive. The couple kept it in the garage for the next time they flew in.

She killed the engine on the snowmobile some distance from the house. There were no other homes around, one of the benefits of this affluent community. No one wanted neighbors. At least not ones they could see from their houses.

The snow was deep on this side of the mountain. She'd brought snowshoes for the last part of the hike up to the house. Strapping them on, she grabbed her canvas bag and started up the mountain. The moon had come up and now poured silver over the snowy landscape.

Sid could see her breath. The house sat on the side of a mountain at about six thousand feet above sea level. She stopped to catch her breath and look back down the mountain to where she'd left her snowmobile. Nothing moved in the darkness of the pines.

Ahead, moonlight shone a path to the house. Sid listened. Hearing nothing but her own breath, she headed for the house.

In and out. She set her watch. Five minutes. Then

she slipped in through the back door that had been unlocked for her by Maisie at the precise time. She knew
exactly where the painting she needed would be hanging and, turning on her penlight, headed right for it.

The exchange didn't take more than a few seconds.
She put the painting into the large canvas bag, remembering the night before when the other bag she'd used
had a hole in it. Another mistake. She was getting
sloppy. Not because of overconfidence, she told herself. No, it was that she'd done this so many times it
was becoming routine.

She thought of Laramie Cardwell as she locked the
door behind her, texted Maisie "Lunch tomorrow?"—
their code—and headed for her snowmobile. As she
drove the snowmobile toward her cabin, she realized
that once she had the painting she'd lost last night,
she'd be done with these kinds of night jobs.

It filled her with a strange nostalgia. She'd been at
this for several years now. When she'd started, she had
questioned her sanity. Why do this when it could go
so badly if she were caught?

Last night that had almost happened. Unfortunately,
it wasn't in her nature to leave anything undone—even
if she *hadn't* needed the painting to finish what she'd
started. She would get that painting back and end this
once and for all.

"So what do you think?" McKenzie asked as Laramie
used his key to enter his new house.

"I love it," he said as he stepped in and took a deep
breath. Through the wall of windows at the front of
the house Lone Mountain glistened in the twilight.

"From what I can tell, he left everything but the art-work—other than the one you bought," she said. He looked around, realizing he would have to get more art for the walls, especially with these high ceilings. Walking through the house, he didn't see much that he would change. Theo Nelson's decorator had done a grand job of furnishing the house.

"He even left dishes, flatware and stemware," McKenzie said shaking her head. "He must not have been very attached to the house." She sighed. "There is a used furniture shop down the valley that we call the Second-Wife's Club. Most of it comes from Big Sky. New wife, all new furnishings. You can get some great deals, if you're interested."

Laramie shook his head. "I can't imagine anything more that I would want or need. It is clear that Theo and his wife didn't spend much time here. Everything looks brand-new. I expect to see the price tags still on everything. Let me get some things from the car and then let's take a look upstairs."

The second floor looked the same except for the study. Theo's computer was gone, but that seemed to be the only change. "He didn't even take any of the books on the shelves," McKenzie commented.

In the bedrooms, the beds were still made up with new linens, down comforters and expensive duvets, she noted. "He left all the linens in the bathrooms and the closets for the entire house."

Laramie glanced around and then headed for the stairs to the master bedroom with the two paintings he had acquired. The room looked much the same, save the spot on the wall where the Taylor West had hung.

He took the painting he'd purchased from Theo Nelson and hung it back where it had been. On the wall next to it, he hung the one his cat burglar had dropped.

He turned on the small spotlights that shone on the paintings and stood studying the two, still unable to find anything to distinguish either of them.

"I'm glad you like the painting," McKenzie said joining him. "I could have gotten the price of the house down another twenty grand without it."

He chuckled. "According to the artist, the original is worth fifty. Your art expert offered me thirty thousand for the one I acquired from my mysterious alleged thief."

She let out a low whistle. "Wow, so you got a deal on both of them. That makes me feel better. But I get the impression you would have paid even more for it and the house."

Laramie smiled. "You did great, McKenzie. I can't thank you enough."

"But which painting is the real McCoy?"

"That is the question, isn't it?" he said. "Meanwhile, I love the house." He walked over to the wall of windows. In the darkness of the winter night, the snow-covered Lone Mountain looked ghostlike.

He stood, admiring his view and wondering when his cat burglar would be back. *If* she would be back. He thought of Obsidian "Sid" Forester and wondered how he could make sure they crossed paths if she didn't come back.

Logic, something he'd always prided himself on, reminded him that he couldn't be sure Sid was his cat burglar.

"Not yet," he said to himself as he looked out at the Montana winter night. But all his instincts told him he'd already found her. Now it was just a matter of catching her in the act.

Chapter Seven

The next morning, after a rough night, Taylor West woke up hungover and upset. He hadn't gotten a moment's sound sleep last night, worrying that he'd been betrayed. Worse if the truth came out…

He picked up his cell phone and saw that it had been turned off. He had four calls from Cody Kent. He listened to the voice messages, then returned the man's call.

Clearly either Rock or Hank had called him—or they both had. And they'd both pretended to him that there was nothing to be worried about. He swore as he tapped in Cody's number.

"What's this about some forgery?" Cody demanded, sounding both angry and worried. Cody related that he'd been by the gallery yesterday and had run into a man with one of Taylor's paintings.

"Laramie Cardwell. I know. He came by my house."

"Was…it…*the*…original?" Cody asked.

"I don't know."

"What do you mean you don't know?"

"I would swear it was."

"So the other one is a forgery. Have you seen it?"

"I know what you're getting at," Taylor said. "The

other one has to be a forgery, right? And anyone could have painted it."

Cody agreed. "So stop getting everyone all riled up over nothing."

"You're right." Still Taylor had a bad feeling about this.

"You'll let me know if there is a reason to worry, right?"

"Of course." He hung up and tried Rock's number. It went straight to voice mail. Where the hell was Rock? He'd gotten off the line so quickly yesterday...

Taylor felt sweat break out under his arms even though his house was cold this morning because he hadn't bothered to turn up the heat.

He'd had a long night to think about it. If anyone had betrayed them, it would be Rock.

LARAMIE HADN'T SLEPT well the first night in his new home. There was nothing wrong with the bed, the Egyptian cotton sheets or the house's ambiance. Still, he'd had trouble getting to sleep. Even after he'd dozed off, he'd awakened often thinking he'd heard something. All night he'd lain in the king-size bed, listening and waiting for the woman to return and thinking about the vehicle that had tried to put him in the river yesterday.

The incident had to have something to do with the painting, right? Which meant it had something to do with the cat burglar. What, though?

Before going to bed, he'd had a thought. Taking out his pocket knife, he'd carefully scratched a very small mark on the back of the canvas on the painting he'd purchased with the house.

He was sure she'd come back for one—or both—of the paintings. He figured if he ever saw them again after that, he'd know which was which. And if she only took one, he'd know which one she'd left behind. He was pretty sure she knew which one was the real one.

With that, he'd turned out the lights and gone to bed. When he'd opened his eyes this morning, he'd half expected to see the paintings gone. He wouldn't have been surprised if she'd sneaked in and taken them both.

But upon waking, he was almost disappointed to see both paintings right where they'd been when he'd gone to bed. She hadn't come for either one. What if he was wrong and she wouldn't be back?

His phone rang. Seeing it was from the marshal, he quickly took the call. "Do you have some news for me?" he said without preamble.

"Yesterday you asked me to check on vehicles owned by Taylor West," Hud said.

"Right. And you told me he didn't own a large brown car."

"No, he doesn't. But his wife, Jade, does. I got to thinking and checked to see if there were other vehicles that might be registered to someone other than Taylor."

"His wife?" Laramie remembered the photograph he'd seen of the pretty young blonde.

"I've put a BOLO out on it," Hud said. "We could get lucky. But why would Jade West—or someone using her vehicle—want to run you off the road?"

Laramie hung up convinced that it had something to do with the painting, but what, he had no idea. As he headed for the shower, he wondered if Obsidian Forester was indeed his cat burglar. The only way he'd know for sure was if she came back for the painting. He realized how much he was counting on it.

Showered and dressed, he went downstairs. He'd just poured himself a bowl of cereal that he'd bought at the store yesterday when the security company he'd called rang his doorbell.

Theo Nelson had a security system but it hadn't gone off the night Laramie had seen the woman on the roofline. Which meant that the woman had disarmed the alarm before entering the house or she had outsmarted the system.

So he wasn't going to bother adding more security. All he wanted were cameras, and nowadays they made such small ones, she wouldn't know she was being captured on video.

He glanced at his watch. He needed to know more about cowboy art. McKenzie had handled everything including changing over the utilities and contacting the alarm company for him. Leaving the security people to do their work, he drove to Bozeman to the Museum of the Rockies. It was another beautiful winter day, not a cloud in the sky, the blazing sun bright on the snow.

He found himself watching his rearview mirror, looking for the large dark car that had run his off the highway the day before. But by the time he reached Bozeman, he hadn't seen it.

Parking near Montana State University, he entered the museum. While known for its dinosaur collection, the museum also held a variety of other exhibits throughout the year, according to the clerk who took his money, stamped his hand in case he wanted to come back later and handed him a map.

Since the museum had just opened for the day, there

were only a handful of people in the new exhibit featuring Old West master artists. There were paintings by both Charles M. Russell and Frederic Remington, two well-known Old West artists from the 1800s.

They had apparently painted what they saw around them, capturing a lifestyle that they romanticized with their art. While four-wheelers had replaced horses at a lot of ranches, his cousin had told him, the cowboy life survived even to this day out here in the West.

Laramie had just stepped into an adjoining exhibition room when he saw a young woman standing in front of a large painting of a Native American chief in full headdress.

It was the same woman he'd seen coming out of Texas Boys Barbecue yesterday. Obsidian "Sid" Forester.

At seeing the woman again, his pulse jumped as excitement raced through his veins. He reminded himself that she was an artist in her own right, so of course she would be here. That didn't make her guilty of being the cat burglar.

She wore jeans and a canvas jacket over a rust-colored sweater. Her coppery hair was tucked up under a Cubs baseball cap, which pitched her face into shadow, making it impossible to see the color of her eyes at this distance. Nor could he get a good look at her mouth. But even in silhouette he could tell that her lips were full.

He remembered the taste of her mouth and felt an ache that had nothing to do with cowboy art. His reasons for wanting to find this woman had gotten all tangled up with a desire to kiss her again. He knew it was crazy and could just imagine what his brothers would say. But he couldn't wait to get his hands on her as if to assure himself that she was actually real. That what she evoked in him that night was real, as well.

Warning himself to take it slow, he moved closer. As if sensing him staring at her, she looked in his direction, then quickly turned away. He felt a start. Was it possible? He wouldn't know until he got a better look, but all his instincts told him he had her.

It DIDN'T TAKE Taylor West long to drive to Gallatin Gateway, a small, almost forgotten town at the mouth of the canyon. Once billed as the Gateway to Yellowstone, the town back then had a train that brought tourists to the beautiful large hotel, before ferrying them into the park.

Rock Jackson owned a small ranch against the foothills overlooking the Gallatin River. The place was run-down, the house small and old with some outbuildings behind it, including Rock's studio.

As Taylor pulled up and got out, he thought he saw movement at one of the front windows. But when he knocked hard at the front door, there was no answer from within.

"He probably saw me and doesn't want to deal with me," Taylor told himself. The drive had sobered him up since he'd been drinking before he'd left home. He hated that the drive might have been for nothing, until he reminded himself that he needed to go to a liquor store anyway.

He pounded again. Still no answer. Moving to peer into a front window, he saw that the place was neat and orderly inside. That made him all the more angry since his own house was a mess. Somehow that convinced him even more that Rock Jackson was guilty of something.

Walking around the side of the house, Taylor noticed Rock's art studio. Was he back there working? Raging inside, now positive that Rock had betrayed him, he stormed toward it. This time, he didn't bother to knock. He grabbed the door handle and turned it. Locked.

Cursing, Taylor cupped his hands against one of the windows. The studio was exactly like something he'd always talked about building on his property. He could see only one painting from where he stood. It appeared to be one of Rock's in progress.

As he started to turn away, he saw that there was another room behind the studio. When he got around back, the door into that part of the building had a padlock on it. That alone seemed suspicious.

He picked up a rock and tried to break the padlock but, failing, tossed the rock away and swore. The mellow he'd had earlier was starting to wear off along with the booze, leaving him with a headache and a worse mood. Furious, he stood outside the studio feeling as alone as he'd ever felt. The temperature had dropped with the appearance of clouds obscuring the sun. He shivered and looked around, not sure what to do then.

He could smell snow on the freezing air and wondered why he hadn't gone south this winter. Jade had wanted to go, but he hadn't wanted to make the long drive to Arizona. Now he wished he had. Laramie Cardwell wouldn't have been able to find him and he wouldn't have known about the painting.

Taylor knew that kind of thinking was crazy. Even if he'd been in Arizona, the painting would have surfaced. He'd seen it with his own eyes. He knew what that meant.

Behind him, he spotted an old barn on the property and walked toward it, thinking he'd look around and wait for Rock to return, since he now realized there was no vehicle here. He didn't want to have to drive all this way again if he could help it.

He pushed open the barn door and stepped into the dim darkness. It took a moment for his eyes to adjust, but he didn't mind. It was warmer in here and with the booze wearing off…

Taylor blinked as a large dark object in the barn took shape before him. At first he couldn't believe what he was seeing. He thought for sure it must have been the beginning of a hangover making him only imagine it.

But there was no doubt. The question was what was his wife's car doing in Rock Jackson's barn?

SID TRIED TO calm her racing heart. Her mind raced, as well. What was Laramie Cardwell doing here? Her first impulse was to flee, but that would be the worst thing she could do. Seeing him here had been so unexpected. She hadn't been prepared. That's why her pulse thrummed and skin prickled at the memory of his touch.

Why *was* he here? Maybe he was simply interested in cowboy art. She groaned silently as she moved from painting to painting, aware of him tracing her steps like a wolf on the scent of its prey.

Wasn't it possible that his interest in cowboy art had been sparked by the painting she'd dropped and nothing more? Which meant he hadn't forgotten about the painting any more than she had.

Was he here trying to find out more about the painting? Or was he looking for her? Her heart took off like a wild horse running in the wind. Was it possible he'd followed her? That thought turned her blood to ice.

Sid prided herself on her quick thinking when cornered—thus the kiss that had gotten her freedom two nights ago. But she was too aware of him—and vice versa. Good sense told her to leave, but she would have to walk right past him. Also, it might call more attention to her.

Even if she was right and this had something to do with the painting she'd dropped... Even if he was looking for her... He didn't know the importance of the painting in his possession any more than he could prove she was the woman he'd tackled that night.

Telling herself to play it cool, she forced herself to relax. She was safe and she had to admit, she was curious about the Texas cowboy. Wouldn't it be to her benefit to learn as much about him as she could? After all, she needed that painting.

As she moved through the exhibit, taking her time looking at each painting, she studied Laramie every chance she got out of the corner of her eye. He was taller than her few stolen glimpses of him had led her to believe. And since he was the business end of the Texas Boys Barbecue empire, she would have expected him to be some computer geek. But the man who'd tackled her had been anything but.

His dark hair was longer than she first thought. Was that designer stubble on his jaw? She smiled to herself, thinking that she might be wrong about him. He might not be as straitlaced and uptight as she'd thought at their first encounter. Either that or he'd loosened up since then.

Laramie moved slowly, studying each painting, stopping longest, she noticed, at an H. F. Powell painting of a cattle drive. The painting was beautiful, a masterpiece. Even someone without an artist's eye would see that.

He seemed so intent that she hadn't realized she'd been caught staring until he turned suddenly in her direction. She quickly swung back to the painting she had been pretending to examine. The intensity of his look had rattled her again. Could she be wrong about him not knowing who she was?

Just as she started to move away, he stepped up beside her.

"I know nothing about this kind of art," he said in his Southern drawl. "Do you really have to be a cowboy to paint it?"

She didn't look at him. "Sorry, but I wouldn't know. I'm not a fan of cowboy art."

"Really?" He sounded surprised. "And yet here you are." She could feel all of his attention on her. "So you just wandered in here like me?"

"It would seem so," she said, and quickly looked at her watch.

"Take this, for example," he said clearly ignoring her subtle attempt to escape. "Is the idea to portray the life of the cowboy? Or romanticize it because these guys look too happy when you know they have to be freezing?"

Sid looked at the painting of cowboys standing around a campfire drinking coffee from tin cups as cattle milled in the background and snow began to fall. He was right. She couldn't help but smile.

Just as she couldn't help looking over at him.

He seemed startled for a moment as he met her gaze. Then his eyes shifted slowly to her mouth. She fought the urge to lick her lips as she recalled his mouth on hers. His gaze returned to hers. She tried not to shiver.

"I know this sounds corny," he drawled, "but I feel as if we've met somewhere before."

She did her best not to react to his words. "If that's your best pickup line—"

He snapped his fingers as if it had only just come to him. "Texas Boys Barbecue. I saw you coming out of there yesterday." While his intent gaze was still probing, his smile was all sincerity. "I'm betting you had the rib special. Tell me I'm right."

She tried to relax. "So you're a betting man?"

He laughed. "Not usually, but then again I'm a long way from home and out of my element. Right now I'm betting that if you agreed to have a cup of coffee with me, it would make this Texas boy feel more at home this far north."

She laughed, as well. "You seem very much at home to me."

"Laramie Cardwell," he said and extended his hand.

Sid felt she had no choice but to shake it. Her hand disappeared into his large, warm, suntanned one. She tried not to react to the jolt she felt. "Obsidian Forester."

"Obsidian? What a beautiful and unusual name."

"That's why I go by Sid."

"Well, Sid, I hope you take me up on the cup of coffee. I haven't met many people since I've been here."

She was tempted, which surprised her. Playing with fire was one thing. Stepping into a blazing furnace was another. Still, he had no way of knowing—let alone proving—that she'd been the woman whose path he'd crossed that night. And if he did suspect, what better way to prove him wrong than by taking him up on his invitation?

Not to mention, he had the painting she needed. Maybe there was another way to get it, other than stealing it outright. Anyway, what would it hurt to have one cup of coffee with him?

Chapter Eight

Violet. It was the color of her eyes. But Laramie realized as they walked the block to the coffee shop that her eyes changed colors in different light. No wonder he hadn't been sure that first night.

But there was no mistaking the lips. They were bow-shaped, wide and full, and a delicate shade of pink today. He'd remembered the feel of them against his the moment he saw them. Crazily, what he'd wanted more than anything right there in the museum was a repeat kiss. He couldn't be sure, with everything that had been happening that night, exactly what he'd felt when she'd kissed him. It had happened too fast. But the next time she kissed him…

Where had these thoughts come from? He reminded himself that she was a *thief.* His plan was to catch her. The chance of there being another kiss was beyond remote.

He was still surprised that she'd agreed to have coffee with him. He'd worried that he'd come on too strong. He'd never been like his brothers, who seemed to all have a way with women. He was more reserved. More cautious, usually. While he'd done his fair share of dating, he'd never met a woman he'd been serious about.

He figured he knew less about women than he did cowboy art, which was saying a lot. So he felt he was out of his league if Obsidian "Sid" Forester was who he believed she was.

"So fess up," he said once they were seated in a small coffee shop a block from the museum. "You did have the ribs, didn't you?"

She had a nice laugh. An amazing smile. The woman was striking from her coppery hair to her heart-shaped face and the row of freckles that graced her cheeks. But it was her eyes that fascinated him. They'd been violet, but now in the winter light coming in from the coffee shop window, they were almost silver. Like a wolf's, he thought. Silver like they'd been in the moonlight the night they'd met.

"You caught me," she said. "I had the ribs. They were wonderful, but I guess I don't have to tell *you* that. I'm betting you're one of the Texas boys."

"Yep. My four bothers and me," he said, figuring she probably already knew that if she'd looked at their story on the back of the restaurant menu. Wouldn't only an innocent woman go to the barbecue restaurant after his encounter with the cat burglar?

No, he thought. This woman was gutsy. She'd go there almost as a dare.

"Barbecue was the only thing we knew, so we started cooking out behind a small house we turned into a restaurant in Houston." He shrugged. "The business just kind of took off."

"What brought you to Montana?" she asked and took a sip of her coffee. He could feel her watching him over the rim of her cup and wondered what game they were playing. She was definitely his cat burglar. He'd stake his life on it. The thought made him think of the car that had run him off the highway. If he didn't stop this, what would happen next?

Laramie knew he should be worried about that. But there was no way he was backing off. "My brothers and I were all born here in Montana. When my parents divorced, Mom took us to Texas where she had relatives. My dad still lives near Big Sky, so one after another my brothers have returned, and each has fallen in love with Montana and a woman... Opening a restaurant up here seemed like a good idea."

"It appears to be doing well. I heard you were opening another one in Red Lodge."

He smiled, nodding. "I handle the business end of it, so it's one reason I'm here, along with wanting to spend time with my family over the holidays."

"So you aren't staying?" she asked and took another sip of her coffee.

"As a matter of fact, I bought a house yesterday partway up the mountain."

"Really?" She didn't sound that surprised. "So you're planning to move up here?"

He shook his head. "I'll only spend part of the year here like most of the residents, it seems. I still own a condo in Houston and operate things from there."

She nodded.

"So tell me about *you*," he said.

Sid shrugged. "Not much to tell."

"Come on, I just told you my entire life story." He took a sip of coffee and asked, "You live in Big Sky." She nodded. "What do you do there?"

Her silver-blue eyes met his. "I paint." Her full mouth quirked into an amused grin.

"Paint?" He pretended to be surprised. "You're an *artist*? Or do you paint houses?"

She smiled as she shook her head. "I'm more of a hobby-craft person. I paint Montana scenes on old rusty things I find like saw blades and old milk cans. I definitely wouldn't consider myself an artist."

"That explains what you were doing at the exhibit," he said studying her. "You really like cowboy art."

"I admire the artists, but cowboy art isn't my cup of tea, trust me."

"What is?" he asked.

The question seemed to surprise her as if no one had ever asked her that before. Maybe that was why it took her a moment. Or, he thought, maybe it took her a moment to come up with a lie. "Abstract. I like lots of color. I prefer impressionism over realism when I paint."

"My sister-in-law McKenzie would love one of your pieces, then." He studied her. She seemed to be relaxed, but he felt a tension just under the surface. He could feel it buzzing like a live wire between them. "I'd like to see your work sometime."

She said nothing as she finished her coffee and looked again at her watch. "I really need to go."

Laramie mentally kicked himself, but he'd never been patient when he wanted something badly. He pushed his coffee aside and stood as she rose. "It's been a pleasure meeting you. I do hope our paths cross again."

"Maybe they will," she said. He could smell the

citrus scent of her morning shower. "Enjoy your new house."

"Speaking of my new house... I am in desperate need of artwork. The ceilings are ten to twelve foot throughout. I have only one painting I'm partial to, but nothing else. With all these walls to fill, I need help. I sure would appreciate it if you could advise me." She started to decline. "Come on, who better than an artist who loves color to help me?"

Don't do it. Sid met the handsome Texas cowboy's gaze. He'd just told her he had only one painting. She didn't have to guess which one that was.

"I doubt we like the same things," she said.

"You might be surprised," he drawled. "I'd love to show you my house whenever you can come by."

"There are plenty of designers around who could advise you on artwork. I'm not the person you want."

"Oh, I suspect you are exactly the person I'm looking for."

She looked at him, wondering how true that was.

"I have a confession," he said leaning toward her. "I have no artistic talent. I'm betting you have a better eye for art than you think. I'd love to see what you come up with."

Was he trying to tell her that he knew who she was? Or that he at least suspected? Or was he hitting on her? That thought almost made her laugh. Wouldn't that be her luck? A good-looking Texas cowboy interested in her and she had to avoid him for obvious reasons.

"You might not like what I come up with," she challenged.

He seemed to study her. "I think I might surprise you."

She feared that was definitely what might happen.

He walked her back to the museum where they'd left their vehicles. A brief thaw had left the streets of Bozeman bare, but there was still plenty of snow in the mountains. Laramie commented on how beautiful it was.

"So do you ski?" he asked as they neared the museum parking lot.

"No." Sid wondered why she'd lied. But then again she was lying just being with this man.

"Snowboard?"

She shook her head.

"You must do something to enjoy winter since you live in Big Sky. Snowmobile?"

He had stopped beside a white SUV. She assumed it was the same one she'd seen the night he caught her leaving Theo Nelson's house with the painting.

"I hate how loud snowmobiles are," she said truthfully and mugged a face. "They ruin the winter quiet, don't you think?"

Laramie smiled at that. "But they seem to be a necessity if you're going to get around in the mountains in the winter and want to avoid the roads."

She looked away. She could feel her heart thundering in her chest. Oh, yes, he suspected her all right. "Don't you ski?"

He laughed at that. "I'm a Texas boy. I doubt I'll be staying here long enough in the winter to learn. But my cousin has invited me to do some horseback riding on her ranch. Do you ride?"

She thought of the horses she'd loved when she was

younger and the many hours she'd spent in the saddle. Surprisingly, she hadn't realized how much she missed it until that moment.

"I love to ride." The words were out before she could bite her tongue.

Laramie's eyes brightened. "Then we have to go for a ride. When are you free?"

"With the holidays and all…"

"I'm staying until after the holiday masquerade ball that I'm told by my cousin Dana I can't possibly miss." He eyed her openly. "You don't happen to be going?"

She shook her head. "I wouldn't be caught dead there." And this time bit her tongue.

He laughed again. "I feel the same way, but my cousin is very persuasive. Listen, I'm serious about that horseback ride and about your help with artwork for the house."

"Speaking of being very *persuasive.*" Their eyes locked for a moment and she felt a warning chill sprint up her back. *Be careful.* This was not a cowboy to fool with. Admittedly, he definitely had his appeal. She recalled the jolt she'd felt when she'd shaken his hand, not to mention the strange reaction to the kiss. "I'll think about both."

"Do that. This is mine," he said motioning to the SUV. "It was nice meeting you, Sid. Oh, I should tell you where I live in case you take me up on my offer. It's the three-story one off Lone Mountain Trail. You probably know it, right?" His gaze met hers and held it. She felt a shiver wind its way up her spine. One minute she was convinced he was hitting on her and the next she was positive again that he knew exactly who she was and was setting her up. "Why don't I give you my phone number in case you can't find it."

"I'll find it," she said as she turned and walked away, mentally kicking herself for this cat-and-mouse game she was playing since she was the mouse and the cat was a much craftier adversary than she'd first thought.

As she climbed into her vehicle, she warned herself to let it go. But that meant letting the painting go. She couldn't do that, she thought with a curse. And Laramie Cardwell was practically daring her to come steal it.

"WHAT IS GOING ON with you?" his brother Austin demanded when he showed up at Laramie's door later that afternoon.

He gave him a confused look. "I bought a house?" Motioning his brother in, he headed for the kitchen.

"*This* house?" Austin said from behind him as he closed the door and followed him. "The house where you saw what you believe was a cat burglar? I know what you're doing and I don't like it."

Laramie laughed. "You're the one who encouraged me to buy a house up here." He opened the refrigerator and offered his brother a beer.

Austin declined with a shake of his head. "I'm not talking about the house and you know it. Hud told me that someone ran you off the highway."

"Just some crazy driver," Laramie said, wondering how much Hud had told his brothers. Apparently nothing more than that since Austin didn't ask him about Taylor or Jade West.

"Is this just about the woman?" Austin asked instead.

"I didn't buy the house for that reason." *Well, not completely*, he thought as he closed the refrigerator. "Come take a look. You'll have to admit the house is perfect for me."

Austin stepped into the living room, still looking skeptical.

"Check out the view," he suggested as he walked to the front window in the living room area. "Open concept. Granite counters. State-of-the-art appliances. What's not to like?"

His brother looked out at Lone Mountain glowing in the afternoon light and seemed to relax a little. "It's nice."

"There are two more floors. The second floor is great for company, two bedrooms, another living area, another bath. The master is on the third floor."

"Where is the painting?" Austin asked.

Realizing there would be no getting rid of him without showing him the painting, Laramie led the way up to the third floor. "Check out the view from here."

"Impressive." But clearly he'd come to see the painting.

The painting was where it'd been when he moved in. And now the alleged original was hanging next to it.

"That's what all the fuss is about?" his brother asked, clearly not that impressed by the artwork.

"It's cowboy art."

Austin shot him a look. "I'm aware of that. What is the original worth?"

"Fifty K."

His brother's eyebrow shot up. "And you bought it with the house?"

"I got a deal on it."

"Not if it's the forgery," Austin pointed out. "Now you have *two* of them?"

"Unless Hud catches the cat burglar and needs them back for evidence."

Austin gave him a "knock off the bull" look. "You think she'll be back for it." Laramie said nothing. What would be the point since it was obvious Austin knew him too well? "Have you considered just how dangerous this might be?"

"I've already found the thief."

His brother's eyebrow shot up. *"What?"*

"I met her today at a cowboy art exhibit in Bozeman. We had coffee."

Austin shook his head as if trying to clear it. "You need to go to Hud and—"

"Without proof? Not a chance. Also I don't want to scare her away." Laramie headed down the stairs.

"So how do you plan to catch her? That is what you're doing, right?" his brother asked, catching up with him.

"I asked her to help me decorate the house."

"Why would you do that?" Austin let out a curse. "If you're right and this woman really is a criminal, then you are in over your head already. I'm serious. What has gotten into you?"

"Isn't it possible that I know what I'm doing? Just because I've always been the brains behind the business doesn't mean I can't do what you and Hayes have been doing for years."

Austin ignored the part about "the brains behind the business."

"Damn it, Laramie, you aren't trained for undercover work."

He leaned against his kitchen counter. "What about the times I've helped the two of you on cases? Give me a little credit."

"At least tell me what you're planning to do."

"I need to know what her game is. She's been seen leaving other houses, but nothing according to the owners was taken. Don't tell me that doesn't intrigue you."

Austin frowned. "I smell a scam, either with the artist, the owner of the painting and/or your cat burglar."

"I have no idea, but," Laramie said, smiling, "I hope to find out."

His brother seemed to run out of arguments. "What is this woman's name? I'll run a background check on her and see if she's had any arrests or convictions."

"Thanks, but I'd rather—"

"Your instincts aside, you need to know who you're dealing with. Unless you don't want to know the truth because... You haven't fallen for this woman, have you?"

"Of course not," he said and looked away, remembering the kiss.

"Laramie—"

"I just don't want you getting involved."

Austin sighed. "How did this woman get under your skin so quickly?"

Laramie shook his head. There was no denying it. Sid had gotten to him.

"If this is about proving something to yourself or to the rest of us—"

"Maybe it started out that way," Laramie admitted. "But if anyone can understand getting hooked on a case, it should be you."

His brother rubbed his neck for a moment before he smiled. "Apparently you are a lot more like me than I ever realized. Okay. All I'll do is run a background check on her. Just let me do that. Unless you're afraid of what I'm going to find out."

"Her name is Obsidian Forester. But I don't want you going to Hud with this yet."

"We'll keep it between us, for now. Obsidian Forester. With a name like that, I shouldn't have any trouble. In the meantime, be careful. You're sure she isn't the one who ran you off the road?"

"I can't imagine how she could be." That was at least true enough.

Chapter Nine

Sid looked around her cabin at all the work she had to do. Since coming back from the museum and her encounter with Laramie Cardwell, she'd gotten little done. Nor had she slept well last night. All her instincts told her to forget about the painting Laramie Cardwell now had in his possession.

If only she could. The painting was a loose end, one she had to take care of, which meant she would have to deal with Laramie Cardwell.

She kept rerunning their conversation in her head. She wavered between, *he knows it was you* and *he can't possibly know* and *even if he does suspect you, he can't prove it*.

Still, getting closer to him—and the painting—felt like a trap. She had no doubt that she could steal the painting back. He would be spending some of the holidays with his family. It would be the perfect time to take it.

But then he would know that, as well. Her head hurt as she considered what he might be up to. If he suspected who she was, then he would try to get proof. She couldn't shake the feeling that he was just waiting for her to show up in the middle of the night to try to retrieve the painting she'd dropped so he could catch her red-handed.

Was Marshal Hud Savage in on it? She didn't think so. Since none of the paintings were missing, he wasn't apt to think that a crime had been committed.

So what was Laramie up to besides tempting her? The fact that he seemed to be tempting her for more than the painting unnerved her. During coffee a couple times she'd caught him looking at her as if…as if he was interested in her? Of course he was, but not because he was attracted to her. And yet, she had felt an electric spark between them. A stirring she hadn't felt in a very long time—if ever.

The thought made her laugh. If it wasn't complicated enough, she could never fall for a *businessman*. She bet that most of the time he wore a three-piece suit and spent his time behind a desk. Definitely not her type. And yet that image didn't quite seem to fit Laramie Cardwell.

No one who spent all his time behind a desk was in that great shape. No, when she closed her eyes, she saw him in boots, jeans and a Western shirt. He'd mentioned going horseback riding. Maybe she would take him up on it and see just how "Western" he really was.

The idea had too much appeal. If she were smart, she would keep her distance. But then how could she find out what he was up to, let alone get the painting back?

She picked up her keys before good sense could stop her and headed for her SUV. It was time to pay Laramie Cardwell a visit.

AUSTIN RAN THE name Obsidian Forester the moment he reached his computer at the small office he kept at his wife's gallery.

"You look awfully serious," Gillian said from the doorway.

"Laramie's met a woman."

She chuckled. "And that's bad?"

"It depends on whether or not she's a convicted felon or worse."

"There's something worse than a convicted felon?"

Austin watched as the information came up on the computer screen. He knew what he'd been expecting. A record that showed the woman was a thief, a forger... at the very least a con artist.

"Well?" Gillian asked as she came into the room.

"No record. Nothing."

"Why don't you sound relieved?"

Austin raked a hand through his hair. "He's my little brother."

"Maybe the woman is fine."

"Maybe she is just starting her criminal career and my little brother is her first victim."

"It sounds to me like you're just looking for trouble," Gillian said as she turned to leave.

LARAMIE HEARD THE sound of the vehicle coming up the road. Another of his brothers? They'd always been protective of him because he was the youngest. He hadn't minded, liking that they had watched his back. But this was different. This was something he wanted to handle himself.

He sighed as he looked out and was pleasantly and

unexpectedly surprised to see Obsidian Forester's older-model blue SUV coming up the road. He hadn't expected her to take him up on his offer—let alone so soon.

Hurrying upstairs, he stashed the painting she'd dropped that night in the closet and then rushed back down. He would show it to her, but not right away.

As the blue SUV pulled in, his heart jumped in his chest with expectation. Even though he knew she was probably only here because of the painting, he still smiled to himself as he watched her get out of her vehicle from a window.

Laramie ran a hand through his thick dark hair and braced himself to see her again. Chimes filled the house as she rang the doorbell. He hoped that the reason Austin hadn't gotten back to him yet was because he hadn't found out anything worrisome about Sid. Bracing himself, he opened the door.

Sid looked out of a fur-trimmed hooded coat. Her face glowed from the cold and the afternoon light. Her breath came out in white puffs, her eyes clear blue like the ice on the river. Snowflakes danced in the air around her. She was a winter wonderland vision standing there.

"Did I catch you at a bad time?" she asked as a few moments passed without either of them speaking.

He mentally shook himself out of his reverie. "Sorry, you looked so…"

"Cold?" she suggested with a smile.

"Exactly, come on in." He stepped aside to let her enter.

"I probably should have called."

"Except you didn't take my number. But your timing couldn't have been more perfect. Let me take your coat. I have a fire going in the fireplace if you need to warm up, and I can make some coffee."

"Thank you," she said, shrugging out of the coat. Her ginger hair was loose and now fell around her shoulders in a sunset wave of color. Her freckles seemed to stand out even more on her pale face. "It's Montana in late December." She shrugged as if being a little cold was expected.

"So you're used to winter," Laramie said as he hung up her coat in the closet by the front door. "I never asked you if you're from here or a newbie like me."

"New to this town. But I was raised in Montana not too far from here." She followed him into the kitchen.

"So where exactly are you from?" he asked as he poured her a mug.

"I grew up outside of Maudlow," she said with a laugh. "You've never heard of it, right? It's to the north. Not much of a town there anymore." She glanced around. "Nice house."

"Thanks. I didn't want anything too big, but by my condo standards, this place seems huge. It does make me want to stay here more, though."

"You aren't planning to stay long this time?" she asked as she wandered into the living room, then turned. "Do you mind?" she asked nodding toward the stairs.

"No, please. Take a look around. As you can see, the walls are all bare down here." He followed her up the stairs, again noting how fluidly she moved. Also how quietly.

On the second floor, she made a lap through the main room, then headed up the second set of stairs to the master bedroom. To the casual observer she didn't seem to know the house. But it was clear to him that she knew exactly what she was looking for.

On the third floor, she entered his bedroom slowly. Fortunately, he'd made the bed this morning and he hadn't left any clothing lying around. Because he'd been expecting her. He was pleased that he'd been right. In fact, she'd shown up even sooner than he had hoped.

She stepped in, seeming to take in the view before she turned first to the right, then slowly to the left as if leaving the painting till the last.

Laramie had to smile to himself. This is what she'd come to see, he thought, as she took in the painting. Everything else had been pretense—he was sure of it.

"This is the painting you told me you bought from the owner?" she asked without looking at him.

"That's it. There was just something about it, if you know what I mean."

"No. Like I said, I'm not a fan of cowboy art, but as long as *you* like it…" She glanced around. Looking for the other painting?

"I'm not sure what I like, to tell you the truth."

"Isn't there art in your home in Houston?" she asked as if actually interested.

"I bought the condo new. It came decorated."

She shook her head as if she couldn't imagine doing something like that.

Her eyes were darker in his bedroom, a deeper blue. He wondered what color they would be when she opened her eyes in his bed in the morning. The thought shook him to his boots. Of course he was attracted her. What red-blooded Texas boy wouldn't be? But to think that there was a chance they might be lovers…

"What's funny about this painting," he said, drawing her back to it, "is that I have two of them."

That definitely got her attention. "Why would you buy two of them?"

"Good question, since, when I visited the artist, he told me he painted only one of them," Laramie said as he stepped past her to open the closet and pull out the second one. He hung it next to the first. "So which one is the original?"

She looked at them for a moment. "I have no idea."

Sid strangled back the cry that rose in her throat. Only moments before she had been looking at all the wonderful wall space he had in his house, thinking how fun it would be to fill it with art. She'd been excited about the ridiculous thought of helping him. How she would have loved it. She had tons of ideas. Not that it would ever happen, but it was fun to fantasize about a lot of things when it came to Laramie Cardwell.

Then he'd said he'd talked to Taylor West about the two paintings, and all the air had rushed out of her. The room suddenly felt too hot, too small, too bright.

She'd barely been able to get the words out. "You showed the work to the artist?" He nodded, hopefully unaware of how upset she'd become. "I would think he would know his own artwork," she said carefully.

"I thought the same thing. Apparently one of these is the original. The other, a forgery. A very good forgery."

"That's remarkable. Did he have any idea who might have been able to forge it?"

Laramie shook his head. "West said the only man good enough to have done the work was one H. F. Powell. Have you heard of him?"

She could only nod.

"But apparently he's dead. So it remains a mystery. Just between you and me? What makes it all the more crazy is how I came to have both paintings."

Sid listened as he told her what she already knew. "That is quite the story," she said when he finished.

"It's a mystery."

"I'm sure you'll solve it," she said, hoping she was wrong.

"Maybe," he said meeting her gaze. "I'm sure hoping I do."

Sid reminded herself that the only reason she'd come over here was to get the painting back, which meant getting closer to Laramie Cardwell. But being here with him, standing this close to him, looking into those blue eyes...

She felt a small tremor move through her. *He knew.* It was time to quit kidding herself. He was just waiting for her to make a mistake. But that wasn't all she saw in his eyes or felt being this close to him. Some kind of chemistry was arcing between them and he felt it, too.

Sid tried to convince herself this was about nothing more than foreplay, flirtation. But the attraction was so strong between them that there was no denying it.

Worse, she *liked* him. Look at the interest he'd taken in Western art since the first night they'd met, she thought with a hidden smile. He'd become intrigued, just as she had become intrigued by him. She couldn't say that about most of the men she'd dated. Her last serious relationship had been in high school. Fortunately she'd been smart enough not to marry him.

But whatever feelings she might have when it came to Laramie Cardwell, the question now was how far she would go to get the painting back.

LARAMIE SAW THE WAY Sid was clutching the coffee mug in both hands. "Your coffee must be getting cold. Let's go back down. I want your opinion on that big wall in the living room."

He'd noticed the change in her. What he'd told her had upset her. But by the time they reached the kitchen, she seemed her cool, calm self again.

This woman would be the death of him. The thought surprised him as if it was a warning. But there was no denying whatever was going on between them under the surface. It wasn't his imagination. This woman did things to him. That alone made her dangerous—not to mention the fact that she was a criminal. A thief. Or worse.

He told himself he wouldn't be stupid enough to let her steal his heart.

"If I'm going to help find the right art for you, then I'll need to figure out what you like," Sid said after he'd warmed up her coffee and showed her the large, high-ceilinged wall in the living room.

"How do you suggest doing that since I don't know what I like?" he asked, inexplicably still intrigued and attracted by this woman. He really had to be careful. Austin was right. He had no idea what he was getting into.

She smiled as she looked up at him, her eyes locking with his. "I guess we'll have to spend more time together so I get to know you better."

He felt a dart of desire puncture his already weak reserve. *She was flirting with him.*

"I completely agree," he heard himself say, all the while reminding himself who he was dealing with. Austin was afraid this woman was dangerous. His brother had no idea given the mix of emotions Sid evoked in him.

She smiled. "Any suggestions?"

She *definitely* was flirting with him. Laying some sort of trap for him?

He decided to play along. "We could start by going horseback riding, but it's supposed to snow this afternoon."

Sid laughed. "I love riding in the snow, but if you—"

"No, I'm in. Just let me call my cousin Dana."

TAYLOR WEST TRIED his wife's cell phone number again. It went straight to voice mail—again. Only this time, the message said that her voice mail was full.

He slammed down the phone. Since seeing Jade's car in Rock Jackson's barn, he hadn't been able to sleep—except for the hours he'd drunk so much that he'd passed out.

"Don't do anything crazy," fellow artist Hank Ramsey had told him. Taylor hadn't wanted to tell anyone, but he was going out of his mind, so he'd called Hank for advice.

"Don't do anything *crazy*?" he'd demanded after hearing Hank's advice. "Rock has stolen my *wife*! And who knows what else he's done." He'd stopped short of telling Hank what else he suspected Rock Jackson of doing. Did he trust either Rock or Hank? Not anymore. Not since he'd seen the painting Laramie Cardwell had in his possession.

"You don't know for a fact that Jade is with Rock."

"Her car is parked in his barn," he'd said between clenched teeth. "And he has a room behind his studio with boarded-up windows and a padlock on the door.

"There could be another explanation than the one you've jumped to."

"What would that be if it was *your* wife?"

"Jade could be storing her car there. Didn't you say she was planning to go to Ohio to visit her sister for a while?"

"Indiana to visit her mother." He'd cursed under his breath, sorry he'd called Hank. "I thought that was where she would go. She never said—it doesn't matter where she went. *Her car is in Rock's barn.* Even if she flew to Mars, why would she leave her car with him?"

"Probably because she didn't want to pay the overnight fee at the airport. Gateway isn't that far from the airport. Rock probably gave her a ride."

He hadn't thought that Jade knew Rock that well. True, she'd been to enough cowboy artist conferences that maybe she'd come to know the artists better than he did. He spent most of his time at those things getting to know the bartender rather than listening to the bull the other artists were spouting.

"Also, I'd be careful about making any accusations since you have no proof about anything. You might want to watch the booze, too. The one thing we have to do is stick together."

Taylor had heard something in the man's voice. Was he warning him? "*I'm* not the problem."

"We don't even know there *is* a problem."

Hank wasn't talking about Jade any longer. "You didn't see the painting," Taylor'd said, trying to keep the anger and the fear out of his voice.

"I'll talk to Rock. I'm sure there is nothing to worry about."

Right, Taylor thought as he went to unlock his gun cabinet.

Chapter Ten

On the way to Cardwell Ranch to meet Sid and go horseback riding, Laramie's cell phone rang. It was his brother Austin.

He braced himself as he took the call. "So what did you find out about Sid?" he asked, just wanting to get it over with.

"*Sid?* You're using her nickname already?" Laramie could practically see his brother shaking his head.

"So did you find something or not?"

Austin sighed. "She appears to be squeaky clean. No arrests, no speeding tickets, nothing. She lives alone, owns a small, older cabin back in the woods outside of Big Sky and drives an older-model SUV." Not a large dark car. "No debt. Makes a modest living with her artwork."

Laramie wanted to laugh with relief. "So why don't you sound happy?"

"Because she's *too* squeaky clean."

"There is no satisfying you, Austin," he joked.

"You still think she's the woman you saw that night with the painting though, right?"

"I'm not sure." He knew he was hedging because he was starting to like Sid—and he *could* be wrong about her being the woman. It had been dark and she'd been wearing a ski mask. All he'd seen were her eyes, and there were a lot of women with blue eyes, right? But those lips… Not every woman had those.

"Just be careful. If you need my help…"

Laramie thanked his brother and drove on to Cardwell Ranch, where he and Sid had agreed to meet. Sid hadn't arrived yet, but his cousin Dana was waiting for him.

"So you've already met someone?" As they stood in her warm, ranch kitchen, Dana sounded too happy to hear that it would be a woman going riding with him.

"You're responsible for marrying off all my brothers, aren't you?" Laramie joked. "Well, this time you've met your match. Marriage is the last thing that is going to happen with this woman."

"I hope you don't have to eat your words," Dana said smiling.

"You'd *better* hope so."

She suddenly quit smiling. "This isn't the woman you caught with the painting?"

"That stopped your matchmaking cold," he said with a laugh.

"You're going horseback riding with *her*? Does Hud know?"

"We don't know for sure that it is even her. Also your husband is convinced this whole cat burglar thing is nothing more than a hoax."

"Well, *I'm* not convinced. What if the woman is dangerous?"

Laramie laughed. "You sound like Austin. Look, if I don't make it back from the horseback ride, you'll have your answer."

"I don't think that's funny."

"Dana, it's just a horseback ride. If you want to worry…she's helping me purchase art for my new house."

His cousin looked aghast. "You be careful, Laramie Cardwell. I've been through enough with your brothers. I don't need you getting into trouble."

Outside, the ranch wrangler had saddled two horses. Laramie told his cousin he was more than capable of saddling his own horses, but Dana had insisted he come inside and visit with her while he waited for his "date" to arrive. Sid had said she needed to run some errands and would prefer to meet him at the ranch.

As a blue SUV pulled into the yard, he went out to greet her. Not surprisingly, Dana followed on his heels.

"Sid, this is my cousin Dana Cardwell Savage. Dana, Obsidian 'Sid' Forester."

Sid held out her hand. "It's a pleasure to meet you," she said. "Thank you for offering the use of your horses. I'm looking forward to it."

"You ride?" Dana asked.

"I grew up on a ranch and rode every day for years."

Laramie noticed that Dana seemed to soften toward the woman, ranch woman to ranch woman. "Then I am especially glad you're going to get to ride today," his cousin said. She turned to Laramie. "How far were you planning to ride?"

"Not far," he said. "We'll be back in a couple hours."

The wrangler handed each of them their reins. Laramie watched Sid swing up into the saddle. Clearly she was comfortable on a horse. He followed suit and they headed along a trail that followed the river. Fresh snow rose in the air around them as they rode.

The day was crisp and cold. Ice crystals hung in the

air and the promise of snow rode on the breeze. But it felt good to be back in the saddle. Laramie had ridden often on his brother Jackson's place. He'd missed it since Jackson had sold his ranch in Texas and moved to Montana.

"Your cousin seems nice," Sid said as they rode.

"Dana? She's amazing. She's also responsible for getting us all to Montana."

Sid cut her eyes at him. "She seemed a little worried about you."

"She's overprotective when it comes to family. But I could tell she liked you. Wait until you get to know her. She's great."

WAIT UNTIL YOU get to know her. He made it sound as if they would be spending a lot of time together. Sid said nothing as they rode through snow-laden pines. Water rushed under the thick aquamarine-colored ice on the Gallatin River beside them. The air smelled of snow. She could see that it was already snowing on the top of Lone Mountain across the narrow river valley.

Was she wrong about Laramie's suspicions? Maybe he really was attracted to her and wanted nothing more than a date.

"I was surprised to hear you'd grown up on a ranch," he said.

"Why is that?"

"You don't like cowboy art."

She chuckled. "You think they go hand in hand?"

"I guess not."

"What about you? Where did you learn to ride?"

"We had relatives with horses when we were young. Then my brother Jackson bought a small ranch. I used to ride there almost every day. I've missed it. I've missed my brothers since they've all moved to Montana. Even my mother is here now."

"You're so lucky to have such a large, close family."

He looked over at her. "You don't?"

She shook her head. "My mother died when I was three. My father passed away some years ago. He taught me—" she hated the tremor she heard in her voice "—to ride."

"I'm so sorry for your loss. It sounds like you were close."

Sid just nodded, afraid to speak for fear she would cry. It surprised her, all this emotion. Let alone the fact that she had opened up to Laramie—the last person she should be letting her guard down with.

"You don't have any siblings?" he asked.

"An older sister who travels a lot."

"You must get lonely," he said glancing over at her.

Catching a whiff of Laramie's fresh-from-the-shower scent, she felt a longing wash over her. But it was more than a desire to be in this man's arms. It was a need to trust someone other than herself. For just an instant, she wanted to tell him everything. What a weight that would be off her shoulders to confide in someone. To confide in this strong cowboy.

As if sensing the way she was feeling, Laramie reined in next to her. It happened so fast that she didn't have time to react. He reached over and she felt his thumb on her cheek. Until that moment, she hadn't realized she'd been crying as he smoothed away a tear.

His gaze locked with hers as he leaned into her, his mouth finding hers. She tasted the saltiness of her tears and the cold scent of the winter day on his lips. Her own lips parted as she leaned into the kiss. He cupped her face, the kiss sweet and soft, then more demanding. She felt heat run like hot water through her veins, warming her to the toes of her boots.

As if realizing what he was doing, he pulled back suddenly. "Sorry. I couldn't help myself."

She swallowed, desperately wanting to grab the collar of his winter coat and pull him into another kiss. His mouth, warm against hers, had kindled a flame in her like nothing she'd ever felt. She ached to lose herself in this man, which was so not like her that it terrified her. She was always careful. But at this moment, she wanted to throw caution to the wind and let her heart have what it wanted.

"I'm not sorry," she heard herself say, although she knew she should be. Did she have to remind herself how dangerous it was to get too close to Laramie Cardwell, of all men?

It was the second time they'd kissed, she realized with a start. Was that why he'd kissed her? If so, then did he now know she was his cat burglar?

Now what? she wondered as they rode back toward the ranch house. Was he setting her up for a fall? After that kiss, she feared she had a lot more to worry about than the painting.

ROCK JACKSON OPENED one eye to see the time on the clock beside the bed. He'd forgotten for a moment where he was. Then he remembered. He was hiding out in a friend's condo in Bozeman and he wasn't alone. He groaned pleasantly, surprised that he'd slept this late. Even more surprised that he could be this happy.

Rolling over, he looked into Jade West's young,

beautiful face. He couldn't believe she was in his bed. The hours they'd spent making love since she'd shown up at his door were a blur.

The moment he'd laid eyes on her the first time at an Old West Artists Conference, he'd been smitten. The worst part that first time was realizing that she was that old fart Taylor West's trophy wife. He'd said then that the marriage wouldn't last.

And he'd been right. But he never thought he had a chance with her. He was more than surprised when she'd shown up at his door and had fallen into his arms. The satisfaction that gave him was shameful, but he still enjoyed every moment of it. Jade was *his*.

Her lashes fluttered and a moment later her green eyes opened. She smiled, making him laugh with delight.

"What?" she asked as she rolled over onto her back. She had the best rack he'd ever seen and this morning she was displaying it for the world.

"I'm just happy." Happier than he had ever been. With two bad marriages and an imminent divorce, he'd had his share of heartbreak. Jade was his compensation for those hard times. It didn't hurt, either, that he'd stolen that smug SOB Taylor West's wife.

"I need to call Taylor."

Her words burst that moment of pure joy. Like a soap bubble, it popped right before his eyes. "Is that necessary?"

She turned onto her side to look at him again. "I need to *tell* him."

"You could let me do that."

Jade shook her head, her delightful lower lip protruding as she said, "I have to do it myself. It's the right thing to do. I don't want him thinking I'm coming back."

She was young, Rock thought. Barely legal to buy alcohol in Montana. What did she know about these things? "He isn't going to be happy. I'm sure he'll beg you to come back. Or threaten to kill us both."

"He wouldn't do that."

Rock wasn't so sure about that. Taylor could be a loose cannon when he was drinking—which was most of the time. Worse, there was bad blood between them and had been for years.

"You don't have to do it *right* now, do you?" he asked as he pulled her to him.

She purred in his arms and he felt his happiness level rise again. He had what he wanted. Well, almost. He was tired of feeling second rate because of Taylor West. Now that he had Jade, he told himself that nothing could stop him from getting what he deserved. He had Taylor's wife. Soon, she would have Taylor's money.

Life was perfect. Almost. After a quick shower, he checked his emails and found the message from Taylor about the painting.

DANA HAD A pot of chili and a pan of warm-from-the-oven corn bread ready for lunch when Laramie and Sid returned from their ride.

"You can't say no, Sid," Dana insisted as they handed over their reins to the wrangler. She stood on the porch wearing an apron, her hands on her hips. "Hud doesn't think he can make it home for lunch, the kids are with their aunt Stacy. I desperately need adult conversation."

Laramie glanced at Sid. She looked torn. He'd felt

so close to her on their ride, but then he'd felt her pull away again as they'd neared the ranch house. Now she looked as if she wanted to run—and yet was tempted to stay. He might have wondered what she had to fear if he hadn't already known.

"Chili and corn bread," he said. "Did I mention that my cousin is a great cook?"

"I would love to," she said to him, "but I can't. Thank you so much. It sounds wonderful," she called to Dana on the porch. "But I have to go. Thank you again for the horseback ride. It was lovely."

Laramie watched her head for her SUV. The kiss had confirmed what he already knew. Obsidian "Sid" Forester was his cat burglar. There was no doubt now. "Maybe I'll see you later?" he called after her, wondering what would happen next. He knew what he wanted to happen.

She smiled and nodded. "Maybe."

"Well?" Dana demanded once the two of them were seated, chili and corn bread in front of them.

"I don't know what to tell you," he said honestly.

"You don't have to tell me anything. The look on your face says it all," Dana said with a grin. "The woman has gotten to you."

He wanted to deny it but didn't bother. "She told me she lost her father some years ago. I can tell that she is still hurting over that. Apparently, he was all the family she had other than an older sister who travels all the time."

"Oh, that's awful," Dana said, sounding close to tears. She knew what it was like to lose someone she loved. She'd lost her mother, Mary, a few years ago and then, because of a dispute over the ranch, nearly lost her sister and brothers. "I wish she'd stayed for lunch. You should invite her to the masquerade ball."

"I already mentioned it to her."

"And?" Dana asked hopefully.

"She wasn't interested."

"I'm sorry to hear that." He could tell that Sid's refusal had surprised her as much as it had him. "Well, *you* have to come. Don't even try to get out of it," Dana said. "We're all going, including all of your brothers. Everyone wears a costume and doesn't remove their masks until the stroke of midnight. It's the biggest event in the canyon."

He cringed inwardly just as he had the first time Dana had mentioned it. "Like I told you before, I'm not much on—"

Dana shook her head. "I'm not taking no for an answer. Believe me, you don't want to get on my bad side."

Hud laughed as he walked into the kitchen. "Trust me, she is so right about that," the marshal said as he bent to give his wife a kiss. "Whatever she wants you to do, just do it."

Dana slapped playfully at her husband as she said, "I thought you couldn't make lunch."

"I got to thinking about your chili and corn bread," he said with a shrug as he helped himself and joined them.

"I was just talking to Laramie about the masquerade ball. Now that he is going to own a house here…"

"You bought that house?" Hud asked he sat down at the table.

Laramie nodded.

"Did your brothers ever admit to playing that trick on you?" the marshal asked.

"Tag swears they know nothing about a cat burglar. Any news on the vehicle?"

"What vehicle?" Dana said. "Did something happen?"

"Some fool ran Laramie off the highway yesterday," Hud said, keeping his head down as he ate.

"What? And this is the first I'm hearing about it?" Dana demanded.

"I didn't mention it because I thought you would overreact," Hud said. "Seems I was right."

"Are you all right?" Dana demanded of her cousin.

"You can see that he is all right," Hud said.

Dana shot him an impatient look. "Why would someone run you off the road?"

"The person must have been drinking," Laramie said. He felt Dana look from him to her husband as if sensing there was more to the story.

"As to the vehicle," Hud said to him. "Haven't found it yet." He took a bite of chili and chewed. "Ever see the woman again?" he asked after a moment.

Dana shot Laramie a conspiratorial look and gave him a slight shake of her head.

"You haven't had any more sightings?" Laramie asked, avoiding the question.

Hud shook his head. "Fortunately not. I have enough problems with whoever is behind the counterfeit twenties floating around. I got a call earlier from the gas station. Someone passed off another bogus twenty. Once they start circulating…"

They ate in silence for a few moments. "I can't wait to throw a housewarming party for you," Dana said.

"Give him a break, sweetheart," her husband said

with a laugh. "You're going to scare him away with all this talk of parties."

"Well, be thinking about your costume for the ball—and a possible…date." She gave him a sly wink. "I promise you, you don't want to miss the masquerade party," she said, undeterred. "I'll write down the name of a local costume shop. You'll want to get yours soon."

Hud ate quickly and went back to work. Laramie stayed to help Dana with the dishes even though she protested.

"Why didn't you mention the horseback ride with my possible cat burglar to Hud?" he asked Dana.

She laughed. "Hud would have just turned into his marshal persona and started asking a lot of questions you clearly can't answer."

"Austin is already doing that."

"Exactly," she said, eyeing him thoughtfully. "Anyway, as far as we know she hasn't committed any crimes, right?"

He nodded.

"Also, I can tell that you're smitten with her. I liked her. Your brothers told me that you've dated a lot but haven't found *the one*. I guess time will tell with Sid, won't it? I hope she changes her mind about the ball."

"I don't see her doing that. She said she wouldn't be caught dead there."

Dana shuddered. "Those were the words she used?"

"It's just an expression," he said, seeing that Dana was now upset.

"Maybe it's for the best. Every year at the ball there's a silent art auction of several paintings to help continue funding the event," she said slowly. "Last year they were local watercolors. This year they are three works by cowboy artists."

"Who are the artists?" Laramie asked as his interest was piqued.

"Rock Jackson, Taylor West and H. F. Powell."

UPSET WITH HERSELF, Sid drove through Big Sky and turned on the road back to her cabin. She had let down her guard with Laramie. What was wrong with her? She knew what her best friend, Maisie, would say about it even before her friend answered her call.

"I kissed him again."

"You *what*?"

"Well, he kissed *me*, but I kissed him back."

"Sid. How did this happen?"

She told her about the horseback ride. "He caught me at a vulnerable moment. I was talking about…about my father dying and—"

"You went horseback riding with him and told him about your father? Have you lost your mind?"

"I only told him that my father had died." Sid sighed. "He could see that I'm clearly not over it."

"You need to be more careful. If you're right about him suspecting you…"

"I know, but there is something about him that makes me think I can trust him when I'm with him. And when he kissed me…"

"It didn't feel like a kiss from a man who was looking for an art thief?"

"No," Sid said with a groan. "It felt like kiss from a man whose reasons were strictly carnal. And I liked it," she cried.

Maisie laughed. "You know what you need, don't you?"

"If you are going to say a man—" As she pulled up beside her cabin she saw tracks in the snow where someone had walked along the back of the property. The tracks disappeared behind the house. "I have to go. If I don't call you back in five minutes…"

"I know what to do," her friend said solemnly.

Stuffing her cell phone into her pocket, she opened her glove box and pulled out the gun. Dropping it in her other coat pocket, she opened her car door and stepped out.

The snow crunched under her feet, a sign that the temperature was dropping as snow drifted down from a blinding white sky. She'd heard that another winter storm was coming in and was surprised it hadn't hit sooner.

Instead of going in the front, she walked along the side of the cabin to the back and looked toward the woods where the fresh boot prints in the snow had apparently come from. She saw a snowmobile parked some distance from the cabin. She could still smell the exhaust. Whoever was inside hadn't been here long.

Her hand in her coat pocket, her finger on the trigger, she opened the door and stepped in.

Chapter Eleven

Laramie had always been the sensible one. He was the brother the others came to when they had financial questions. He was the one who tried to keep them out of trouble. He was the one—though the youngest—they all expected to be the rational, clear thinking one.

Given what had happened in the past few days, he shouldn't have been that surprised to see that all four of his brothers were waiting for him when he returned to his house. He suspected they hadn't come to see his new residence as he got out and walked toward the waiting vehicle—and his waiting brothers.

"I hope you brought me supper from the restaurant," Laramie said as his brothers all piled out of Austin's SUV. "And more beer." None of them even smiled. He braced himself for the lectures that he knew were coming as he opened the front door of the house.

"Why don't we all have a cold one?" he suggested as he walked into the kitchen. Behind him, they all trudged in, stopping to take their boots off at the door. He turned around to stare and then laugh.

"What's so damned funny?" Jackson demanded.

"All of you. You're all so well…trained now. Is that what marriage does to you? If so, I'll pass."

"Don't try to change the subject. You're in enough trouble," Hayes warned.

"I'll take that beer you offered," Tag said. The other three brothers shot him an annoyed look. "Hey, we can lay into him and still have a beer while we do it."

"If this is about Sid…" He opened the refrigerator and brought out five bottles of beer.

"We just heard about someone running you off the highway in the canyon," Hayes said. "You didn't even bother to tell us?"

"I'm fine," Laramie said. "But I appreciate your concern," he said as he handed them each a bottle.

"Where have you been?" Austin asked, sounding as though he was interrogating one of his suspects back when he was a deputy sheriff in Texas.

"At Cardwell Ranch having lunch with Dana and Hud," Laramie said, twisting off the cap from his beer. He took a drink, then added, "Before that I went on a horseback ride."

"Alone?" Austin asked, then sighed when Laramie said nothing. He wrenched the top off his bottle of beer. "I told you to be careful. A horseback ride?"

"You probably want to see the house," Laramie said. He was still too happy about his afternoon ride with Sid to want to argue with his brothers. Not that he didn't understand their concern. He was too smart not to realize he was playing with fire.

"I want to see these damned paintings," Tag said. He looked toward the stairs. "Are they up there?"

"They were when I left," Laramie said.

SID EASED HER FINGER off the trigger of the gun in her coat pocket. Her older sister stood over the painting on her easel—after having picked the lock on Sid's back door. Sid tried to tamp down her annoyance. Seeing her was like seeing a ghostly image of herself. People used to think the two of them were twins. They looked that much alike, especially when Zander had gone strawberry blonde.

The fact that they were half sisters wouldn't have surprised anyone to see them together—same father, different mothers. But few people knew they were even related because Zander was always gone and they were never seen together.

"Zander, what are you doing here?" Sid hated the edge to her voice. But from past experience, she feared a visit from her half sister didn't bode well.

Zander turned and smiled. "Merry Christmas!"

She slipped out of her coat and hung it on the hook by the back door. "You're here for *Christmas*?"

"Don't sound so surprised," her sister said, stepping to her to give her a hug. "We've missed too many holidays. I decided not to let another one go by without spending it with my little sis."

She caught a whiff of her sister's favorite perfume, a scent that transported her back to their teen years. It also reminded her that it was Zander who'd taught her about breaking and entering. And that was the least of Zander's crimes.

"So you just happened into the area, grabbed a snowmobile and decided to visit?" she asked as she stepped back from the hug.

Zander sighed. "You've always been so suspicious. I came by snowmobile because it had been too many years since I'd gotten to ride on one and I wanted to surprise you. Clearly, I did. Come on, we're all the family we have left."

"And you thought after several years of me not hearing from you that you'd just stop by and surprise me," she repeated.

Her sister laughed and shook her head. "Sid, in case no one has told you, it's *Christmas*. I've heard families get together, exchange presents, sit around the Christmas tree and drink eggnog. At least that's what they do in movies," she said, glancing around Sid's cabin. "But it certainly doesn't look like Christmas here. Where's the tree and the eggnog, the stockings hung with care?"

"If I'd known you were coming for a visit—"

"Not to worry. I'll take care of everything, including filling up your refrigerator. Sid, what do you eat…? Or do you?" She continued, not expecting an answer apparently. "You look thin. I hope it's because you're painting and not because of that crazy quest you've been on."

Sid didn't want to talk about either with her sister. "Where have you been this time?" Zander had taken after her mother, a model who'd disappeared a few years before Sid was born. Her sister had apparently picked up that wandering gene.

"I tend to follow the sun. You know me," Zander said noncommittally as she moved around the cabin. "Unless, of course, I get a hankering to spend Christmas in Big Sky with my sister."

Zander couldn't seem to let grass grow under her feet. According to their father, the photographs she'd seen of Zander's mother hadn't captured her wild spirit. Her father, who'd loved women to distraction, had moved on at fifty after Zander's mother had left, and had another child sans marriage. Even though Sid's mother was younger than he was, he'd managed to outlive her by twenty years.

"I don't have an extra bedroom," Sid said, unable to turn her sister away, "but you can take mine and I'll—"

"I already have a place to stay. I didn't come to move in. Or to keep you from your…work. But don't make any plans for Christmas Eve. I'll bring everything."

Sid looked at her sister and felt that old blood bond between them as well as the memories that would always link them. Her timing was questionable, but it *was* almost Christmas, wasn't it? It had been too long since she'd even seen her sister—Zander was right about that. Also, they were the last of their family and the last link to their father.

Sid hugged her again, harder this time while silently praying her sister was telling the truth about her reason for being here now. "I've missed you, Z."

"THE PAINTINGS ARE identical right down to the picture frame," Hayes said as he studied them. "I would swear they were painted by the same artist."

"I took the supposed forgery to an art expert. He offered me thirty thousand for it and offered to document it as the original," Laramie said. "Even the artist who painted it believed this was the original. At least at first."

"Are you sure the one you bought with the house isn't the forgery?" Jackson asked. "McKenzie says most forgeries are easy to spot. All you have to do is look at the colors, the brushstrokes, the canvas…but this one…" He shook his head.

"It is perplexing," he admitted. "But there is a certificate on the back claiming it is an original and one of a kind. That was good enough for its original owner."

"Something isn't right," Hayes said, looking worried. "Either the artist painted more than one of these and lied, or this is a masterful forger. What about the other houses where this…cat burglar was seen?"

"Hud said the owners checked their artwork," Austin said. "It hadn't been taken."

"That's why the marshal thinks the whole thing is a hoax," Laramie pointed out.

"Except you caught the woman and have a second painting that is identical or damned close," Austin said. "If she's switching the originals for forgeries, she has one profitable scam going, and so far she's gotten away with it. Which means she can't let you keep this painting." He glanced over at Laramie and swore. "That's what you're counting on, isn't it?"

"Or maybe the artist is in on it," Hayes said. "You said you talked to him?"

"Taylor West seemed as perplexed by it all as I was," he said. "But according to him, he's the top moneymaker with his art. So if you were going to forge anyone's, it would seem smart to copy his."

"You were run off the road after you visited this Taylor West?" Austin asked, clearly knowing that was the case.

"Coincidence," Laramie said, shrugging. Austin mugged a face at him.

"Whoever is doing this is good, really good," Hayes said studying the artwork.

Laramie nodded. "I asked West who he would

suspect of forging his work. The only artist he could think of who was that good was H. F. Powell."

"I've seen his work," Jackson said. "He was one of the originals like Charles M. Russell and Frederic Remington. But didn't I hear that he's dead? Unless he forged this painting before he died…"

Laramie had thought of that. "What do you know about him?"

His brothers all shrugged.

"I just know that one of his paintings is going to be auctioned off at the ball," Tag said. "McKenzie expects it to go for a lot of money because there aren't many of them around. Most of his work was lost in a house fire the night of his death. Apparently he was a character. I guess in his old age, he locked himself in his studio and no one saw him again. He died destitute with what would now be hundreds of thousands of dollars worth of his paintings going up in flames with him."

"The paintings all burned?" Laramie asked.

"McKenzie said the fire turned out to be arson. The old man apparently started the blaze himself."

"What about the one being auctioned off at the ball?" he asked.

"Apparently it was one that he'd sold before his death," Jackson said.

"I WAS HOPING you'd be glad to see me," Zander said, pretending to pout. "After all, I taught you everything you know."

"Not *everything*." Zander had taught her how to pick locks at a young age, how to break into houses through windows and not leave any evidence. She'd taught her how to steal—and how to get away with it.

For that she owed her since that talent had certainly come in handy.

But fortunately, Sid had learned other things that had helped her in life that her sister could have benefited from. Everyone in Big Sky thought she had no siblings. She'd kept Zander a secret for reasons she didn't want to admit. Now she regretted that—and the times she'd wished it was true.

"So what have you been up to?" her sister said, studying her. "Is there a man in your life?"

Sid shook her head and turned away. "Why would you ask that?"

Zander laughed. "Because you're young, somewhat attractive," her sister joked since she was clearly aware how much they resembled each other, "and this place is crawling with rich men."

Sid groaned. "We're not all looking for a sugar daddy." She wondered now where her sister was staying. It would be just like Zander to have met some man who was letting her stay in his guesthouse—if not his master bedroom.

"Well, don't wait too long to find one," her sister said. "It gets harder as you get older."

Sid started to point out there was only seven years between them. But in the bright light reflecting off the snow outside, Zander looked as if the years they'd been apart had taken a toll on her. Her sister lived hard and fast as if that, too, was in her genes.

Zander walked around the cabin, picking up things and putting them back with no apparent real interest. "So are you almost finished with your diabolical plan?"

She sighed and gave her sister an impatient look. "Diabolical?"

Zander shrugged. "You are almost done, though, aren't you?" She turned to look at her. "You have all the paintings?"

"Not quite."

Her sister nodded. "Then what?"

"I really don't want to talk about this with you. Like you said, it's nearly Christmas. Let's not dig up the past."

Her sister looked angry for a moment, but then nodded. "You're right. We never agreed on much anyway, but we are still blood. Daddy would have wanted us to be friends."

The mention of their father brought tears to Sid's eyes. He was the one person in their lives they could agree on. They had both loved him in their own ways.

"I'm not here to keep you from your...work. But if I can help, you'll let me know. I might be a little rusty at the undercover stuff, but I doubt it would take much to bring it back." Zander grinned. "In fact, I'd welcome the diversion. Life has been too tame for too long."

Sid doubted that. "You didn't seem to have any trouble breaking into my cabin."

Her sister waved that off with a laugh. "Hardly a challenge. You really should consider getting better locks. You don't even have a security system," she said, looking around the small cabin and frowning. "Which means you don't keep anything you value here."

Sid had wondered how long it would take her sister to get to the heart of the matter. But she ignored it, determined not to discuss this with her. "If you're coming back Christmas Eve, I should tell you I don't like eggnog. But if you still remember how to make nachos like you did when we were kids…"

Zander's smile never reached her eyes. "Got the message."

Sid doubted she did. Before the holidays were over, her sister would return to her real reason for being in Big Sky. In the meantime, she wondered what her sister might be up to and asked as much.

"I thought I'd do some skiing and maybe lay around in the hot tub at the place I'm staying."

Sid said nothing, but that didn't sound like the sister she'd known and loved. Since she was fourteen Sid had pretty much been on her own. Growing up with a father who worked all the time and a sister who was a thief, she had learned to take care of herself—any way she'd had to.

Unfortunately, Zander, the firstborn to the mother with the movie-star looks, had been pampered as a child—until her mother disappeared. After that, Zander had merely taken whatever she wanted—including any money she could steal from their father and, finally, the ranch itself.

"I have to run, but I'll be back Christmas Eve with bells on." Zander laughed as she left, her perfume lingering along with the good—and bad—memories she brought with her.

Sid listened to the sound of the snowmobile's motor as it died away in the distance. She couldn't let Zander jeopardize everything she'd worked so hard for. Sinking into a chair, she put her head in her hands and fought tears of anger and frustration. As much as she loved her sister, she couldn't trust her. That alone broke her heart.

She thought of Laramie Cardwell. This house of cards she'd built felt as if it was about to collapse around her. But she had no choice. She had to get that painting back from him. And, knowing her sister, she had to stop Zander from whatever she'd come back to Montana to do.

Chapter Twelve

Later that day, Sid stopped by the grocery store to pick up a few things. She couldn't be sure that she would ever see her sister again—that was until she got a call from someone that Zander was in trouble.

But she would buy a few groceries anyway, just in case. She couldn't depend on Zander not to show up Christmas Eve with only bells on.

Pulling a twenty from her purse, she handed it to the clerk. When the clerk hesitated and began to inspect the bill, Sid felt a chill race up her spine. In that instant, she realized that she couldn't be sure she'd had a twenty in her purse this morning.

With a groan, she also realized that she'd gotten out of the habit of checking her wallet when her sister was around. But it wasn't like Zander to take money and leave change.

"I'm sorry, but I can't take this bill," the clerk said as she motioned for her supervisor to come over.

Sid could feel her face heat with embarrassment as other customers began to stare at her. Her stomach roiled. "What is wrong with the bill?"

The clerk didn't answer. It wasn't until the marshal showed up that Sid learned she'd somehow picked up a counterfeit bill.

PARKED IN THE trees so he could see Rock Jackson's driveway, Taylor West checked to make sure the gun was loaded as he waited. He thought about his wife and took another pull on the bourbon bottle. Jade had called earlier.

"Where are you?" he'd asked as nice as he could the moment he answered.

"Bozeman," she'd said in a small, guilty voice.

He'd hoped Hank might be right about Jade leaving her car in Rock Jackson's barn so she wouldn't have to pay to leave it at the airport. Instead, she was still in the state? Only miles from home?

"What are you doing there?"

"Taylor, I have some news that might upset you," she'd said in that innocent voice she used when she needed money—or now wanted something much worse.

"You think?" he'd asked sarcastically. "I found your car in Rock Jackson's barn."

"*What?*"

"Don't tell me you didn't know it was there."

"Taylor—"

"Jade—"

"She's leaving you, Taylor," Rock had said after taking the phone. "I wouldn't try to fight her, if I were you. From what she's told me, she has more than enough grounds for a divorce. To avoid all the bad publicity, you would be smart to give her what she wants." With that, the bastard had ended the call.

What had Jade told Rock? The mere thought sent Taylor back to the quart of bourbon he'd picked up at the liquor store. The quick swig hit his stomach like a hot brick. He tried to remember the last time he'd eaten. He'd been a mess ever since Jade had left and now she was leaving him for good? Leaving him for Rock Jackson? Had she lost her mind?

On top of that, he'd heard that Rock Jackson had been spending money as if he had it. Taylor was familiar enough with Rock's art career to know that the money hadn't come from the sale of his paintings.

Taylor had a pretty good idea where the money had come from, the lying, cheating bastard. Rock hadn't just stolen his wife, he was jeopardizing everything.

He told himself to be patient as he waited for Rock and Jade to return. He turned on the car radio to keep him company. A holiday song began to play on the radio. With a groan, he realized Christmas was only days away. "Merry Christmas," he said bitterly as he turned off the radio.

Rock would have to come home at some point. He laid the gun in his lap, took another swig of bourbon and listened for the sound of an approaching vehicle.

When Taylor woke up, Rock still hadn't returned. Now almost sober, he started the engine and drove home, determined he would be back, though, tomorrow.

SID WAS ONLY a little surprised to find her sister waiting for her at the house. Zander had let herself in, of course, and was unloading into the refrigerator groceries that she'd apparently picked up in Bozeman.

"I was questioned by the marshal today," Sid said as she brought in what she'd purchased after the marshal had let her go.

Zander lifted a brow in alarm. "Does he know—?"

"No, not about that. Seems I picked up a counterfeit twenty-dollar bill somewhere. You wouldn't know anything about that, would you?"

"Me?" Zander slammed the refrigerator. "Why is it that no matter what happens, you are always suspicious of me?"

Sid laughed. "Yes, why is that? You haven't been in my purse?"

Zander turned to roll her eyes. "You know me so well, do you? Can you imagine me getting into your purse and *leaving* money? This...plot of yours has clearly destroyed your common sense."

"Stop trying to change the subject."

"Why? Don't you think it's time that we had a talk?" her sister said, coming back into the room and plopping down on the couch. "Come on, sit down and tell me what's going on. Remember when we used to talk for hours."

"About the boys you had crushes on," Sid said going into the kitchen and putting away the perishables she'd purchased. As she finished she looked into the living room at her sister.

Zander smiled at her as she patted a spot beside her on the couch. "You can talk to me. Clearly something is bothering you." Her sister cocked her head at her. "You sure there isn't a man? I've never seen you so... off balance."

That her sister knew her so well bothered Sid more than she wanted to admit. She didn't think she was that easy to read. Clearly, she was wrong. Laramie threw her off balance. He made her heart beat too fast. He destroyed her common sense, because she'd actually been thinking of telling him the truth about the painting— and why she so desperately needed it back.

Sid sat down on the couch, curling her legs under her, remembering, not the times she'd had to save Zander, but the times her big sister had saved her. When had the tables turned? When they'd lost their father during those months before his death?

"What would you like for Christmas?" Sid asked, not wanting to confide in Zander about Laramie or anything to do with her so-called quest.

Zander shook her head, looking disappointed. "I didn't come back for presents."

"Why did you?"

Her sister rose to pace the cabin floor. "Isn't it possible I wanted to see you?" She turned to stare at her. "Isn't it possible I was worried about you?" Sid hoped that was the case. "You think you know me, Sid? Well, I know you."

That was what scared her.

"I wish I could trust you, Z," she said, speaking her innermost wish at that moment and then wishing she hadn't.

Zander smiled as she sat back down and took one of Sid's hands, squeezing it. "I guess I'm going to have to prove it to you."

"I'm sorry I thought you'd put the counterfeit twenty in my purse." She actually had thought Zander had switched it for a good twenty. "I probably picked it up somewhere without knowing it."

"See?" Her sister was all smiles. "So while you're in this trusting mood—"

She pulled her hand free. "Z, if this is about money—"

Her sister laughed. "I love it when you call me Z. It's been too long. But I wasn't going to ask for money. I was going to offer my help on your…project."

Sid eyed her. "I thought you were against it."

"Not really. I thought it was dangerous, a waste of your talented time. I didn't see the point. And, while I'm being honest, I felt guilty for making things even harder for you before Dad died. But you've brought me over to your side. You're almost done, right?"

She nodded, studying her sister, wondering if she could trust this. But she felt herself weaken. She had adored Z growing up. She'd missed their connection in the years since.

As much as she didn't like to admit it, Laramie Cardwell *had* become a problem. Her own fault. She shouldn't have gotten this close to him. That had been foolhardy—and dangerous.

But she wasn't quite ready to ask for her sister's help in dealing with him.

WHEN ROCK AND JADE finally came up for air the next day, they left the condo where they'd been staying. Rock hadn't thought far enough ahead as to what they would do now. He'd been in a state of happy delirium, but now that he'd come out of it, he began to worry.

Since her talk with Taylor, Jade had seemed upset, making Rock all the more nervous. For a while he'd been able to forget about his soon-to-be-ex wife, Carla. She'd been looking for ammunition in the divorce. It was one reason he'd borrowed his friend's condo. He'd been so careful not to give her anything she could use against him—until Jade had turned up at his door.

All he could hope was that Carla didn't get wind of this until the divorce papers were signed. She knew he didn't have any money, but she wanted everything else, including his family ranch. He'd told her he would see her dead first.

But now that Jade would be able to take half of

Taylor's money according to Montana law, he was willing to give Carla everything just to get his freedom. That would take care of that problem.

Unfortunately there were other things to be dealt with. He hadn't liked hearing that Taylor had been on his ranch and had found Jade's car in the barn. What else had he discovered? Had he been looking for Jade? Or something else?

He tried not to worry as he looked over at Jade and counted his blessings. She was every man's dream. Jade had modeled for lingerie catalogs, so maybe she wasn't a supermodel, but she was a beauty. He'd been jealous of Taylor from the first time he'd seen them together. Everyone knew the only reason she was with that old man was his money and fame, two things that had ruled Rock out from the get-go.

But then there she'd been, standing on his doorstep and then crying in his arms. It hadn't taken a lot to get her into his bed, once he'd assured her he would help her take Taylor to the cleaners in the divorce.

What he hadn't thought about was his own life. What was he going to do with Jade now? If only his divorce was already final. What if Carla was at the house waiting for him? She'd rented a house up Bear Canyon but she often stopped by the ranch without warning. How was he going to deal with her with Jade on his arm? It could get ugly fast.

Also, he realized belatedly, he needed some time to clear out a few things at his house. Now that he had Jade and, soon, Taylor's money, he would be making some changes—more than just getting rid of Carla. But it would be better if Jade never found out how he'd been able to live the past six months.

He looked over at her, realizing he would have to drop her off somewhere. He couldn't take her home.

"I have an idea, a treat for you to make you feel better while I take care of some things," he said.

She looked at him expectantly. She'd been moody since talking to Taylor. She wouldn't be thinking about going back to the old fool, would she?

"I know of this great day spa."

That picked up her mood considerably. Jade liked the finer things in life. Nothing wrong with that, he thought.

"I don't have any money," she said in that little-girl voice he thought charming.

"My treat." He smiled over at her as he drove toward the day spa. "I'll pick you up later and we'll go see this lawyer I know."

"Don't you think I should talk to Taylor before I talk to a lawyer?" she asked. "Maybe he won't fight me on the divorce."

"Baby, trust me. He isn't going to let you go without a fight. That's why we need to beat him to the punch." He just hoped Taylor wasn't hitting the bottle. No telling what the man would do then. "Trust me, Jade. I'll take care of you." *And you'll take care of me,* he thought.

She leaned over to kiss him on the cheek. "I don't know what I would have done without you."

"You'll never have to find out."

Jade still had the body of a model. But sometimes, he wondered about what went on in that pretty head of hers. The fact that she'd married Taylor to begin with had always bothered him. Was it just for the money or had she really cared about him?

"Just out of curiosity," he asked as he parked in front of the day spa, "why did you *marry* Taylor?"

She frowned. "I was in Mexico, drinking tequila at this cantina. He came in with a painting he'd just finished. I couldn't afford to buy it, but I really liked it."

"You married him for a painting?"

"That, and he told me he owned a ranch in Montana." She shrugged. "You know what's funny. Once I sobered up, I didn't even like the painting."

Rock laughed as he reached across to open her door. "Maybe half of everything Taylor has will make you feel better about it."

AFTER HER SISTER LEFT, Sid knew she had to end this before Christmas Eve if at all possible. Zander being in town added a new complication to her plan.

It didn't take Sid long to find out what new alarm systems Laramie had installed in his new house. She'd used different approaches to get past security systems in the past. But she'd found the best way was the most direct.

She'd gotten her old friend Maisie French to get a part-time job at the local security company. Almost all of the Big Sky residents used the same firm. She called her now to ask if Laramie Cardwell had contacted her office yet.

"He's sticking with the security system already in place but adding cameras around the house," Maisie said.

Sid laughed. He thought he could catch her on video?

"I can send you the location of the cameras," her friend offered. "Or, if I'm working that night, I can shut them down long enough to let you get in and out." Big Sky in winter was prone to power outages so if the system went out for no more than ten minutes, it wasn't anything anyone would question. Unless of course there was a burglary.

"I thought you had a rule about going back a second time?" her friend said after Sid told her that she now had no choice but to get the painting back from Laramie Cardwell.

"I know, but it can't be helped. I can't have that painting floating around out there."

"Can't you just offer to buy it?"

Sid laughed. "He's already suspicious—if not downright convinced I'm a thief."

"But right now he has no proof. If he catches you trying to get the painting back…"

"It's a chance I have to take. He mentioned that he has a family thing tomorrow night."

"And you don't think that sounds like a trap?" Maisie cried.

Sid had to laugh again. "It absolutely does. That's why I have to hit his house tonight." She sighed. "But there's another problem—Zander."

Her friend groaned. "Let me guess—she's broke, she needs help, she wants money." Maisie had known her and Zander since they were kids growing up.

"She says she's only in town to celebrate the holidays with me. She's coming over Christmas Eve. That is why I have to take care of this before then."

Maisie groaned. "You don't trust her, right?"

"She's my sister."

"Exactly."

"I have a plan."

"Of course you do." Her friend laughed, but quickly sobered. "Be careful. I don't like this. But since I am the new kid on the block, I'm working tonight. Just let me know what time. And watch Zander."

"I always do. This is almost over."

"And it's no coincidence that Zander shows up now. It's almost as if she…knows."

Sid had thought the same thing. She disconnected and looked across the room at the costume she'd rented along with the mask for the upcoming ball. She'd told Laramie she wouldn't be caught dead at the ball. She hoped she was right.

Chapter Thirteen

Taylor was getting sick of waiting again outside Rock Jackson's home. More than that, he'd run out of bourbon and found himself sobering up for the third day in a row. All of which wasn't good news. Today, he'd been determined to wait for Rock and Jade until the cows came home, if that's what it took.

But he decided a quick run into the packaged goods store to get another bottle wouldn't take that long. It took a little longer than he'd expected because he'd run into a couple of men he knew and they'd bought him drinks, trying to get a free painting out of him.

Sometimes it felt as if everyone wanted a piece of him. He thought of Jade and the first time he'd laid eyes on her. He'd had to have her, no matter the cost. He was no fool. He'd known why she'd agreed to marry him in Mexico. He'd talked up his ranch, his paintings, his fame and fortune. He hadn't had to look at her to see her disappointment when they'd gotten back to Montana. He'd felt it come rolling off her in waves.

Jade had expected a place like out of one of those fancy home magazines. His ranch house was newer but it wasn't as posh as she would have liked. Nor was his fame and fortune up to her standards. Not to mention how quickly she'd gotten bored living in the canyon. She'd spent most of her days burning the rubber off his tires running back and forth to Bozeman.

Marrying Jade had been a mistake. He admitted that as he drove back toward Rock's place. Every bit of his common sense told him to let her go. Good riddance. He could afford to hire a housekeeper to cook and clean for him since Jade hadn't been good at doing either. He would be better off without her.

Except he didn't want Rock to have her.

LARAMIE HAD DONE his best to get Sid off his mind. He couldn't even explain it to himself, but there was something about her.

"What is your attraction to this woman other than the obvious?" Austin had said when he'd stopped by earlier.

"You mean that she's beautiful, intelligent, talented?"

"No, surely it hasn't skipped your attention that we Cardwell men have a weakness for women in trouble."

"She doesn't seem to be in trouble," Laramie had said.

Austin had chuckled. "You don't believe that for a minute and neither do I. Whatever she's up to, I'm betting it's dangerous. You've already been run off the road. Next time, it might be more than a warning."

After his brother had left, Laramie pulled out his phone. "Do you have plans for tonight?" Laramie asked when Sid answered. "I know it's kind of late, but the Cardwell family gets together to decorate cookies and drink hot chocolate, with marshmallows of course, and sing carols."

"Seriously? I can't even imagine such a family."

"It probably sounds awful to you, but I thought if you didn't have any plans…"

"I do have plans," Sid had said. She'd sounded surprised by the invitation. "Otherwise, I would love to."

"Really? I'm glad to hear that. Maybe next year."

"Next year?" She'd laughed. "You can plan ahead that far?"

"Can't you?"

She hadn't answered that.

"Dana also wanted me to tell you that we're having steaks."

"It sounds wonderful, but I can't," she'd said before she could weaken. "Thank you for the offer, though. Please give my regrets to Dana."

"I will. She'll be disappointed. Not as much as me, though," he'd added. "Well, enjoy your holidays if I don't see you before then. Maybe I'll see you after?"

"Maybe."

SID FELT A TIGHTENING in her throat and felt her eyes blur as she thought about his earlier call. She could envision the family in that large living room she'd only gotten a glimpse of through a window.

Steaks at Cardwell Ranch sounded wonderful. But to spend a holiday in that house with that family? There would be music and laughter. Knowing what little she did about Dana, there would be food and drinks. She could almost smell the evergreen tree, almost taste the gingerbread men fresh from the oven, almost hear the sound of Christmas carols being sung by the family.

Laughing at her foolishness, she pushed the vision

away. She'd only seen family gatherings like that in movies and television soap operas. Did they really exist?

She thought of her own childhood and the goofy little tree she and Zander had dragged in one year. They'd made ornaments for it and bought presents to put under it. They hadn't been much. Those had been the lean years before things got really bad.

Swallowing the lump that had formed, she realized she was hugging herself. What would Laramie think if he knew the truth?

She shoved that thought away. For all she knew, the invitation was just him still trying to track down his elusive cat burglar. The invitation was just to let her know he wouldn't be home tonight. The trap was set.

Sid hated being this suspicious. Especially of a man she was developing feelings for. *Did* have feelings for, in spite of the circumstances. The thought made her laugh. She really needed to finish this and move on.

As Rock drove into his ranch, he was glad to see that Taylor's SUV wasn't parked out front. He wouldn't have been surprised if it had been. Taylor could be a hothead. He drove straight to the back of the studio where his car would be out of sight just in case the fool came searching for his wife. He wasn't looking forward to a face-to-face with the artist, drunk or sober. There was too much history between them, not to mention the one big secret that had them locked in a death grip for life.

At the back of his studio, he was surprised to see where someone had beaten on his padlock trying to break in. Had it been Taylor when he'd found his wife's car in the barn? Or his not-ex-enough wife, Carla? He hadn't given her a key. He wasn't stupid.

Opening the lock with his key, he was glad to see that everything was as he'd left it. But the evidence couldn't stay here, not when he planned to bring Jade home with him. He popped open the back of the SUV. He had a storage shed rented in town that no one knew about, not even Carla, since he'd put it in his other ex-wife's name. He was damned glad of it right now.

With any luck, he would never need any of this again, he thought, as he loaded everything into the back of the vehicle. If things worked out with Jade, he wouldn't need to make extra money and could get rid of all the evidence soon. He still couldn't believe his luck.

He tried to relax, to be happy. Hell, he should be celebrating right now. He had it all. Or at least he would soon. But he'd never been one to count his chickens before that last egg hatched. His life had been too tough not to know that things could turn sour at a moment's notice. Especially when dealing with a woman like Jade…

It didn't take that long to load everything and drive down to the storage shed. On the way back, feeling confident he was in the clear now, he had a feeling he'd forgotten something. He swore as he remembered what it was, then he drove back toward the ranch. Glancing at his watch, he told himself to hurry. Jade would be getting antsy. He called her and, sure enough, she was finished and waiting for him.

"Go next door to the bar. I'll be there before you know it."

LARAMIE WAS DISAPPOINTED that Sid couldn't be here with him as he entered the Cardwell Ranch main house. He wondered what her plans were as he made his way to the kitchen where Dana was at work.

"Sid's busy?" Dana asked as she slid warm cookies from a pan onto a cooling rack. "I'm sorry."

"Me, too." Would she take advantage of him being gone and take the painting tonight?

On the drive to the ranch he'd told himself he should cut this visit short after Christmas and return to the warmth of Houston—and the job he was getting paid to do. But watching over the Texas Boys Barbecue empire didn't take much watching. If he was being truthful, the company now had accountants and secretaries that did most of the work. He was more of an overseer. Maybe that was why he'd been getting a little bored with it.

Bored enough that he'd been looking forward to catching an art thief. The only thing worse would be falling for the thief.

His father, Angus, came into the kitchen and slapped Laramie on the shoulder, wishing him a merry Christmas. He hadn't seen his father yet on this trip to Montana. Dana was so excited that the whole family could be together, even Austin, who had been terrible about missing family get-togethers.

"The steaks are about ready," Angus said to Dana. "Hud wanted me to let you know." He took the huge platter Dana handed him and headed back outside.

"Everything else is ready," she called to Angus's retreating back, then turned to Laramie. "I'm sorry. But Sid probably has plans for the holidays, don't you think?"

He had no idea. In the time he'd spent with her, he had learned little about her. His gut told him, though, that she was in trouble, and that alone made him want to save her. It was a Cardwell trait that ran in his family, one he'd never felt so strongly before. Cardwell men were into helping women out of tight spots, he thought, as his brothers, father and uncle came in from the outside grill, followed by a flock of small laughing children.

Laramie had just never experienced what he was feeling for Sid. But now he understood its power. He realized he would do whatever it took to save Sid— even if it meant saving her from herself.

The smell of beef steaks filled the dining room as everyone began to take their seats, the kids all at a smaller table nearby. Laramie tried to enjoy himself, but he couldn't get his mind off Sid. What was she doing right now? He hated to think.

Earlier that day he'd found an article on a famous art forger who was so good that a lot of art experts would no longer authenticate paintings for fear of being wrong. Was there a cowboy artist that good here? Taylor had said the only person good enough was the deceased H. F. Powell.

Laramie barely heard the chatter around the table, the clink of glasses or the rattle of silverware. As the meal wound down, he looked out the window. It was already dark in the canyon even though it was still relatively early. Cardwell Ranch sat at the foot of the mountains alongside the Gallatin River. Earlier he'd driven over a wooden bridge to get here, the entire landscape shrouded in ice-cold white.

"Why do you keep looking at your watch?" Austin

demanded from next to him at the huge dinner table in cousin Dana's dining room. A burst of giggles came from the children's table. Dana got up to see what was going on.

Laramie shook his head. He just had a feeling he couldn't shake. It wouldn't be enough to catch Sid on camera. He needed to catch her red-handed. He needed to see it for himself.

"You need to let it go," Austin said as they all rose to take their dishes into the kitchen. "You need to let *her* go."

Laramie looked at his brother. "What if I can't?"

His brother groaned and shook his head. Austin actually looked sorry for him.

"Tell Dana I had to go," Laramie said, realizing he had only one choice as he handed his brother his dirty plate. "She'll understand."

WHEN HE GOT BACK to Rock Jackson's ranch, Taylor was disappointed to see that they still hadn't returned even though it was getting dark. He settled in again with a new bottle. He'd gotten a quart since he was determined to stay until Rock returned and he'd realized that could take all night.

He kept the gun handy as he parked under some pines at the edge of the property where he could see any vehicle that pulled in, but where Rock wouldn't notice him.

Too much bourbon mixed with lack of sleep and food, and he found he couldn't keep his eyes open. Laying the seat back, he decided to take a nap, telling himself he'd hear Rock when he drove in.

The dream started out nice enough. A sunny, bright

day in summer. He had been for a ride that morning after doing his chores. His father had gone to Fargo, North Dakota, to pick up a bull he'd bought. He'd wanted Taylor's older brother to go along, but Buzz didn't want to go.

"Then you're coming with me," his father had said.

Taylor couldn't think of anything worse than being trapped in a truck with the old man for two days. Not to mention, he'd been the old man's second choice. He knew his father would browbeat him the whole way. He'd always been a disappointment to his father.

On impulse, he had pretended to be sick to his stomach. His father had changed his mind about taking him and left alone. It was perfect. Buzz had some girl he planned to spend all his time with in town. Nothing could keep Taylor from doing what he loved.

He'd retrieved his paints and canvas from under the bed where he'd kept them hidden and went downstairs to the well-lit kitchen. A wave of nostalgia hit him now at the thought of the many hours he used to sit here with his mother when she was alive. She said she loved to watch him paint. She always protected him when his father caught him painting.

"You're making a sissy out of that boy," he would bellow. "I need a ranch hand, not some worthless, namby-pamby kid who likes to paint pretty pictures."

That day, with the sun coming in the kitchen window along with a warm breeze, he'd gotten lost in his art. He was so absorbed in what he was doing, he didn't hear his father return. He didn't hear his footfalls until the man was behind him and then it was too late.

All he felt was the first blow—the one that broke

his arm. He never painted after that. Not until he'd escaped the ranch and his old man.

Taylor stirred, the dream making him moan with pain in his sleep. He blinked. Had he heard a vehicle?

Chapter Fourteen

Sid had little to thank her sister Zander for, and yet tonight as she climbed on her snowmobile, pulling the ski mask down over her face, she was thankful for the part of Zander that loved breaking the rules. Her sister had acquired a talent for breaking and entering at a young age. A couple of times she'd dragged her unsuspecting little sister into her mischief. When Sid had gotten caught, she hadn't told on Zander.

Instead, Sid had used that leverage to force her sister to teach her the tricks. Since then, she'd picked up a few of her own thanks to the internet. That and making the right friends. Her childhood friend Maisie had been quick to help with Sid's plan by coming to Big Sky and getting the job at the security company.

Along with being able to shut off the power to a house for up to ten minutes, Maisie was also able to give Sid computer access to the cameras Laramie had installed. She could see him coming and going that way. Her computer beeped whenever the camera was activated.

Earlier, she'd watched on screen as Laramie came out of the house, all dressed up and carrying a bottle of wine as he got into his rental SUV and left. No doubt headed for Cardwell Ranch. She felt a pang of regret. If only she was going with him. She thought about the horseback ride and the kiss. There was something about this Texas cowboy that tugged at her heartstrings—the worst thing that could happen to her right now.

As she drove her snowmobile up the mountain, she told herself that Laramie Cardwell's only interest in her was as an art thief. If she thought it was more than that—which she wanted to be true—then she was setting herself up for a heartbreak.

Zander had called earlier asking about what kind of wine Sid preferred.

"Seriously?" Sid had said.

Zander had laughed. "So you're still a beer drinker. You're such a Montana girl. Okay. I can't wait for tomorrow night. Maybe I'll drop by a few things I've picked up later tonight. Would that be all right?"

She'd said she had to go out for a while. "But I trust you know how to let yourself in."

Her sister had chuckled. "See you later, then."

Sid hoped she had plenty of time to get this job done and return before her sister showed up. She didn't like the idea of Zander having too much time alone in her cabin.

Taking the back trails she knew so well, she put the Texas cowboy out of her mind. She was on a job. Just business—plain and simple. She would get in and out. And that would be the end of it. If Laramie suspected she was the one who'd taken the painting, well…let him prove it. Not even Laramie Cardwell could seduce the truth out of her. But she would like to see him try, she thought for only an errant moment.

If he was merely trying to catch a thief, then once

she had the painting, he would lose interest in her. It would be over. She'd have the proof she needed about his feelings for her. That thought did little to warm the cold winter night.

She stopped a short distance from the house and killed the engine. Working her way through the snow up to the side of the house, she checked her watch and waited until the outside light behind the house blinked out.

A few moments later, she was climbing up the side of the house onto the roofline. She went in the same way she had the first time—through an upstairs window. She'd disabled the lock the first time she was there and doubted Laramie had noticed. Most windows this high above the ground were never locked anyway.

Lowering herself by the rope she'd attached to the chimney, she dropped down to the window, opened it and slipped inside. As long as she moved quickly, no one would be the wiser. In and out. Five minutes tops.

As she slipped into Laramie's master bedroom, she dropped to the floor and checked her watch. She waited a moment, listening, before she turned on her penlight.

"IT WAS GOOD to see you, son," Laramie's father said as he left. "I hope you think about spending even more time up here now." It was what Angus always said. It was no secret that he hoped all of his sons would return to Montana.

Once outside, Laramie breathed in the cold night air and headed for his SUV. He couldn't shake the feeling that Sid would hit his house tonight. The cameras he had installed would prove it. But he knew that what he needed more than anything was to catch her in the act.

Maybe then he could get some answers out of her. And then he could corral these feelings he had for her.

But it was still early. He told himself she wouldn't attempt the theft until later—just as she had done last time. Laramie knew he was hoping he was wrong about her. Maybe she really was busy tonight—doing something other than robbing him.

It had begun to snow again as Laramie drove toward Sid's cabin. Huge lacy flakes spiraled down from the darkness in a dizzying white. He told himself he was on a fool's errand. He would find her in her cabin wrapping presents, visiting with friends over a bottle of wine, possibly even spending a quiet evening with another man.

That thought jolted him hard. He hadn't even considered that there might be a man in her life. A woman who looked like her? Of course, there would be a man.

Or not, he thought. Wouldn't a man have to know what Sid did late at night? The man would either have to be in on it or…

He found her cabin from the directions the waitress who knew her at Texas Boys Barbecue had provided.

"You can't miss it. Small cabin, stuck back in the woods. It's the last place on that road."

As the cabin appeared in his headlights, he saw that there was no light behind the windows. He slowed, aware that he would now have to turn around. What if she was home…and sitting in the dark, waiting for him to drive by to check on her? He shook off that ridiculous idea.

She wasn't home, he told himself as he turned around. Probably out on a date. Or shopping for groceries. Or out on a date. Or finishing up her Christmas shopping.

Mentally he kicked himself. What was wrong with him? He'd never acted like this with any other woman.

But when he stole a look in his rearview mirror as he pulled away, he knew that Obsidian "Sid" Forester was like no other woman he'd ever met. He also realized as the dark cabin disappeared from view, that it was probably no coincidence that she lived on such an isolated road. He couldn't see any other cabins near hers but it was dark and the pines were thick on the mountain behind her cabin. Maybe this place wasn't as isolated as he thought, but he wouldn't have bet on it.

The snow was falling harder now. It blew past horizontally on a gust of wind, shaking the SUV, shaking his thoughts. Sid wasn't out buying groceries or last-minute Christmas presents. Nor did he believe she was on a date.

No, if he was right about her, she was at his house right now stealing the painting like the thief she was.

JADE CALLED RIGHT AS Rock was pulling around the back of his studio. "I'm on my way."

"Are you trying to get me drunk?" she asked, sounding pouty. "I'm already on my third drink."

Just what he needed—her sloppy drunk before he rescued her. "I forgot to ask. How was the spa treatment?"

"Wonderful."

"Good. Sip that drink. I'll be there in ten minutes." He disconnected, pocketed his phone and got out. Even with darkness upon him, the temperature was in the forties. He loved a good holiday thaw when the snow disappeared at lower elevations and he didn't have to be bundled up as much. He was sick of winters. Maybe he and Jade should move south. They could get a place in Arizona. Jade might like that.

He unlocked the back door of the studio again and stepped in. The room smelled of chemicals and the odor hit him like a two-by-four in the face. He quickly moved to the windows and opened them even though this thaw couldn't last much longer.

Breathing a little easier, he looked around the room for what he might have forgotten. Maybe he was just being paranoid. No, he realized as he spotted it. He'd forgotten to clean up the garbage with the empty bottles of acetone and bleach, masks and gloves. He shook his head at how close he'd come to blowing it. Pulling out a garbage bag, he quickly filled it and spun around as a shadow filled the open doorway.

Alarmed, he dropped the bag. "Oh, you startled me there for a moment." He reached for the garbage bag, telling himself to play it cool. "I was just leaving, but maybe we can talk—" The rest died on his lips as he saw the gun. "Wait a minute." He held the full garbage bag in front of him as if it would stop a bullet, and he took a step back, his mind racing. "This is a mistake. You don't want to—"

The first shot caught him in the chest at heart level. He barely felt the second or third or even fourth shots as he fell to the concrete floor.

LARAMIE DROVE ONLY partway up the mountain to his house. He hadn't seen another soul on the road tonight once he'd left Meadow Village, other than the faint light of a snowmobile through the falling snow shortly after he'd turned around at Sid's cabin.

In a wide spot where the snowplow had turned around, he parked and got out. The walk up the mountain had him breathing fairly hard. Even though he was in good shape, he still wasn't used to the altitude.

As he reached the top of a rise, he slowed. Fortunately there was no moon tonight and clouds obscured even the stars. The darkness would have been complete if not for the blanket of reflective snow that covered the ground.

That gut feeling he'd had earlier at dinner had proved right, he thought as he looked toward the house. A tiny light bobbed in the master bedroom. *Sid was here.*

His heart began to pound with both excitement at finally catching her—and disappointment. He realized he'd been hoping he was wrong all this time. Or that there was a good explanation. Clearly he didn't know this woman. For that reason, he felt a sliver of concern that he might be walking into something more dangerous than he thought.

His plan on the way up the mountain had been to catch her in the act. Now that he was almost to the house, he realized she could be armed. He thought of the woman he'd kissed. She wouldn't shoot him, even if she was armed, he told himself.

You'd stake your life on a kiss? It was Austin's cynical voice in his head. He knew his brother had staked his life on even less.

Laramie reached the side door, unlocked it and stepped in. He had only a matter of seconds to disarm the silent security system. Or had she already disabled it? He couldn't take the chance that it might go off and alert her.

As quietly as possible, he stepped to it to punch in the code and saw that the system was off. He looked toward the stairs.

SID PICKED UP the painting and hesitated. Why had he left both of the paintings here together? Because he knew she would be back for one of them. She slid the light over the canvas of one and then the other until she found what she was looking for.

The difference between the two paintings was impossible for anyone else to discern. But she knew where to look. She picked up the forgery and, her penlight guiding the way, started toward the window with time to spare.

But still her footsteps faltered. Laramie would know she'd taken it. He'd been waiting for her to return. He'd had the cameras installed so he could catch her. She remembered his lips on hers, the taste and feel of him.

She shook off the memory. All the kiss had been was a ruse. Him making her doubt he was onto her. She mentally shook herself, telling herself she had known the score from the beginning. It wasn't as if she'd fallen for it. The irony didn't escape her. She was the thief, the liar, the one who wasn't being honest with *him*.

Sid wasn't sure if she heard or just sensed something.

Someone else was in the house.

She froze, listening. A faint sound two floors below. All houses had their own unique sounds, but this was human.

Her gaze shot up to the cameras. No light. They

weren't on yet. She checked her watch. Time was running out. She had to move.

Hastily, she snapped off the penlight and slipped it into her pocket. As she started to step out the window into the falling snow, Sid belatedly realized the mistake she'd made in her hurry. The penlight, not all the way into her pocket, fell out, dropped to the floor and clattered on the hardwood.

LARAMIE LOOKED UP as he heard the sound. She was here, on the top floor. He felt his heart take off at a gallop at the thought of catching her red-handed. They could quit playing this game of cat and mouse.

The thought should have brought him more satisfaction. Wasn't this what he'd wanted since that first night? No, he thought as he turned toward the stairs. At first all he had wanted was to find the woman—not fall for her. Had he found her in Obsidian "Sid" Forester? He was about to find out.

He took a step toward the first stair, telling himself it would be over soon, one way or another. Behind him, he heard a floorboard creak and frowned in momentary confusion. Until that moment, he hadn't considered that there might be more than one of them.

As he spun around, he had only a moment to take in the person before him. "Sid?" The glare of the falling snow outside the window lit her face. Too late he caught the movement of her arm—and the weapon in her hand.

Instinctively, he tried to step back, bumping into the stairs. The blow to the side of his head staggered him. He fought to keep his balance, but his eyesight was dimming to nothing more than a pinpoint.

He felt himself falling, blackness filling his vision, filling his head. The last thing he saw was her standing over him with the weapon in her hand.

Chapter Fifteen

"You hit him too hard," Sid said with a curse as she knelt down beside Laramie. She hadn't known what was going on downstairs and had been shocked to find her sister standing over him.

"I had no choice. He would have caught you."

Sid quickly felt for a pulse and then checked his pupils. "What are you doing here anyway?"

"I thought you might need my help. When I saw him come by the cabin…"

She shot her sister a look over her shoulder. The last thing she needed was help. In a few more seconds she would have been out the window and gone.

"He saw me," her sister said, raised her hands in surrender when Sid turned to glare at her in disbelief. "Don't worry, he thought I was you."

"Great. That's perfect."

"Maybe he won't remember anything," Zander offered.

Sid shook her head in exasperation as she turned back to Laramie. "Get me a cold cloth out of the kitchen."

Zander returned a few moments later. "Here." She thrust the cold wet cloth into Sid's hand. "So what are *you* doing here?" Her gaze went to the painting leaning against the wall where Sid had dropped it. "Is that one of them?" she asked in a hushed voice.

Sid didn't bother to answer as Laramie moaned, his eyelids fluttering.

"You should get out of here before he wakes up."

"We both should," Zander said, her eyes riveted to the painting. "And why all the concern over this guy? Is there more going on here than even I think?"

"Wait for me at my cabin. We can talk later." Zander still hesitated. Laramie moaned again. "Go! I don't want him catching both of us here."

Her sister finally moved, slipping out into the night. Laramie was coming to.

LARAMIE WOKE WITH a killer headache. He tried to get up from where he lay on the floor, but he settled for sitting on the lower step until his head cleared a little. He had a bump on his temple that throbbed and hurt like hell when he touched it.

At the sound of footfalls, he looked up, shocked to see he wasn't alone. "What did you hit me with?"

"I'm sorry about your headache."

"Are you?"

"How's your head?" she asked, ignoring the question.

"It hurts." He narrowed his eyes at her, trying to understand what she was still doing here. Why hadn't she just taken the painting and left? "I figured you'd be long gone."

She nodded. "So did I." She took a step toward him. "Here, I found these in your medicine cabinet. I'll get you a glass of water." She dropped two white pills into his open palm.

He stared at them.

"They're just aspirin," she said.

"Right."

"If I was going to drug you, don't you think I already would have?"

"Quite frankly, I never know what to expect with you," he said.

He took the two white pills she handed him and stared at them while she went into the kitchen. They looked like two over-the-counter pain pills.

She handed him a glass of water. He met her gaze, held it for a moment and downed the pills and the water.

"So are we going to be honest now?" he asked. When she didn't say anything, he added, "I hope you aren't going to tell me that the real cat burglar was the one who hit me."

"It's a long story."

"One I'm dying to hear."

"Maybe we'd better go into the living room where it is more comfortable, then," she said.

He got up from the step, still feeling woozy, but anxious to hear any explanation she had to give.

"I don't know where to begin," Sid said when they were seated across from each other.

"Why don't you start with why you need that painting so much," he said pointing to it where she'd left it by the stairs.

She sighed and looked away for a moment. When she looked at him again, he saw that her beautiful eyes had filled with tears. "I need it to catch the men who murdered my father."

Laramie felt a start. Her father was *murdered*? "Who was your father?"

"H. F. Powell."

LARAMIE STARED AT HER. "You're his *daughter*? So Forester is your...married name?"

She shook her head. "My parents never married. I told you it was a long story."

His head ached. He rubbed his temples, trying to make sense of this. "You said your father was murdered? I hadn't heard anything about that."

"Because his death was ruled an accident. The investigators believed my father had started the fire that destroyed his studio and everything in it—including him."

"But you think it was murder?"

"I *know* it was murder, and I've been working to prove it."

He sat up a little straighter. While his brain probably wasn't functioning as well as it could have been under the circumstances, he couldn't help suspecting he was being conned.

"Excuse my skepticism, but I don't see how stealing paintings will help you solve his...alleged murder."

"At first, I thought that the investigators were right and that my father *had* started the fire," Sid said. "Until the forgeries started showing up."

"Maybe it's my headache, but I'm having trouble—"

She sighed again and got to her feet to pace. "You have to understand. My father was an eccentric genius and because of that he made enemies." Sid waved an arm through the air as if that was putting it mildly. "Admittedly, he was often his own worst enemy. He wasn't...conventional. He hated rules. Which is probably one reason he and my mother never married. He'd married once before and the woman had left him. My father also didn't make the best husband—or father, for that matter. He would lock himself in his studio for days on end until he was too exhausted to paint."

Laramie said nothing, just letting her talk, as he tried to make sense of what she was telling him.

"When the Old West Artists Coalition was started, my father just assumed they would invite him to join." She stopped pacing to let out a laugh. "He would have turned them down flat. He *hated* organizations. But instead, they shunned him, saying that while his paintings were all right, his character was lacking."

Laramie thought he could see how that might affect a man like the one she'd described. "He was angry?"

Sid barked out another laugh. "He was *furious*. He swore he would show them that he could paint so much better than any of them that they wouldn't be able to tell his forgeries from their own work." She nodded. "He became obsessed. He quit painting his own work, determined to show them up."

"They found out and tried to stop him," he guessed.

"He must have bragged to someone about what he was doing. He planned to expose them at their annual conference."

Laramie saw where she was headed with this. "The forgeries were in the studio the night of the fire?"

She nodded. "I've always questioned why he would go to all the trouble of painting the copies only to change his mind and destroy not just them, but also himself." Sid met his gaze. "That's just it. He wouldn't have."

"So whoever took the forgeries…"

"Killed my father."

Laramie blew out a breath of air as he leaned back. "And you think you know who took them. If you're right, then you do realize how dangerous this pursuit of yours is, don't you?"

She smiled at that.

"Right," he said, feeling foolish. This was a woman who ran along rooflines in the middle of the night, broke into houses, chancing everything to get these forgeries back. This was his cat burglar.

"So have you figured out who is responsible?"

"I suspected it was one of the four founders of OWAC, but now I'm thinking all four of them were behind it. They are the ones who kept my father out of organization, the ones he despised the most. They are the ones who had the most to lose by his plan to expose them and their organization. They'd been pulling some fast ones, using the organization to raise money for charities and pocketing most of it. They had reason to fear him. By then my father was being recognized as a great artist. Once he revealed the forgeries, there would have been a lot of bad publicity that would have hurt them and shone a light on their organization. They would have been lucky if they hadn't ended up in jail."

Laramie closed his eyes for a moment, glad that the aspirin seemed to be doing the job of relieving his headache a little. "What I don't understand is why did the person who killed your father take the forgeries? Why not leave them to burn?"

"I assume the killer was worried that the fire might be put out before all the evidence burned. Maybe they planned to destroy the copies. If I'm right and all four of them were in on it, then one of them must have been responsible for getting rid of the forgeries—but didn't."

Laramie nodded. "You're sure these are forgeries that your father painted?"

"Yes."

He thought about what Taylor West had told him. There was only one artist who was so good that he could make a forgery that even the artist believed was his painting—H. F. Powell. That explained why West got so upset once he realized the significance of the painting Laramie had brought to him. It was one of the forgeries.

"Still, it makes no sense," he argued. "Why would one of them take the chance of letting these forgeries get back on the market?"

Sid shrugged. "Money, would be my guess. Also, maybe he thought enough time had passed that the duplicate paintings wouldn't come to light."

He studied her beautiful face, realizing what she'd been doing. "So you're stealing back the forgeries."

She didn't deny it.

"So you have all of them?" Laramie asked.

"With the one you have, yes."

"And with them, you'll be able to prove who killed your father?"

She looked away. "I thought I would, but it isn't going to be as easy as I'd hoped. And now I have one more forgery that has turned up that I need to get. Unfortunately, I don't have an original to trade."

"WAS THAT HIM?" Zander asked as Sid came in the back door. Her sister was sprawled on the couch, a half-empty bottle of wine on the floor next to her.

She was already furious with her sister. "What?"

"The man you're falling for," Zander said, grinning as she sat up. "Don't try to deny it. I saw the way you were with him." She shook her head. "I can't see any way this is going to turn out well."

"Don't you have somewhere to be?"

"Not really. You never told me why you went there tonight."

She had no patience for this. "Guess."

"Another so-called forgery." Zander shook her head. "I was hoping you had turned into a real cat burglar. I guess it was too much to hope for. Seriously, when are you going to stop this?"

"When I'm finished with what I started. Thanks to you, I didn't get away clean tonight." She turned her back to her sister, too angry to deal with her right now. "I had to tell Laramie what I was doing."

Zander swore. "That was a mistake."

"Maybe." She trusted him, probably a mistake. But she'd had no choice, thanks to her sister.

"If you'd told me what you were doing, I could have helped you."

Sid turned. "*Helped me?* You could have helped by staying away."

"Isn't it possible that I want justice for our father, too?"

"I thought you didn't believe he was murdered?" Sid demanded. Then she saw her sister's expression. "You *do* believe it."

Zander's gaze met hers. "Does it matter? I still can't see how any of this is going to help. He's gone. Nothing you do can bring him back."

She didn't want to argue about this. It wasn't revenge.

It was simple justice. But maybe it would end just as her sister had predicted and she wouldn't be able to prove who killed him—let alone see that the men responsible got what was coming to them.

"Just let me finish what I started."

Zander got up from the couch. "Tonight aside, you're pushing your luck. I don't even want to know what you told Laramie Cardwell after I left. If any of this gets out and the killer finds out you're after him... The way I see it, you *need* my help."

Sid would love to have argued that her sister was wrong. Unfortunately, if she had any hope of pulling off the next part, she could use Zander's expertise.

Seeing her weaken, her sister smiled. "You know I'm good because I taught you everything you know."

"Not *everything*. If I thought I could trust you..."

Her sister looked excited. "Whatever it is, I'm in."

"You might not be when I tell you my plan."

LARAMIE DIDN'T KNOW what to think after Sid left. She'd trusted him with her story. He'd believed her. And while he'd done his best to talk her into going to the marshal, she'd refused, telling him that while she had all the paintings, she didn't have any proof. Yet. She made him promise he wouldn't go to the authorities, either.

"I went to the police when the first forgery turned up," she'd said. "I saw it at a gallery in Bozeman. The police didn't believe me."

"How can you be so sure it was one of your father's?" he'd asked, hating how skeptical he sounded.

She'd gone to the painting she'd left leaning against the wall by the stairs and brought it over to him. "I know this looks identical to the original, but my father had too much ego to copy it exactly. He had to leave his mark on it." She'd cocked the painting so the overhead light fell across it. "It's very small but if you look closely," she'd said pointing to a spot.

"It looks like a wolf's face."

Sid laughed. "Like I said, my father's ego made him leave a little something of himself behind. The lone wolf. But it is camouflaged and easily goes unnoticed—unless you know what to look for and where." She'd seen his still-skeptical expression and had left the painting to go upstairs to retrieve the original. "See for yourself."

He had.

Now he found himself pacing the floor as she had done. He couldn't help being worried about her. Like he'd told her, this was dangerous. It probably explained why someone had tried to run him off the road after his visit with Taylor West. He was reminded as well of Cody Kent's reaction to the painting as well as Taylor's. Had Taylor called Cody as soon as he'd left? He probably called all of the others, if Sid was right and they were responsible for H. F. Powell's death.

"They know now that the forgeries were never destroyed," Laramie had told her. "They'll be running scared and who knows how far they'll go to keep this from ever coming out. It isn't just about ruining their reputations. We're talking murder."

Sid had smiled. "If I'm right, they'll start turning on each other—if they haven't already."

"Or they'll all come after you."

"They don't even know that I am H. F. Powell's

daughter," she'd said with a shake of her head. "But I'll be careful."

He had seen that she was touched that he was worried about her. He had moved to her, cupping her cheek with his palm. "Let me help. Two of my brothers are private investigators and I—"

"No." She'd moved away before turning to look at him again. "I can't tell you how sorry I am that you are involved at all."

"Sid, can't you see that I… I care about you?"

She'd smiled and nodded. "But now I need you to trust me. Can you do that?"

He'd said he could. "But if you need me—"

Sid had stepped to him to give him a quick kiss. "I'm almost finished with this. Any interference now could destroy all the work I've done."

Against his better judgment, he'd agreed to stay out of it. What choice did he have? Go to Hud with what he knew? He couldn't do that to Sid. Nor did he know how to help her—other than letting her finish what she'd started.

Getting to his feet now, he walked into the kitchen and saw the wet cloth on the counter. Frowning, he picked it up as a flash of memory came rushing at him. Sid leaning over him, pressing the cold washcloth to his forehead.

More of the memory teased at him. Sid with something else in her hand, only…only something was wrong. He shook his head, regretting it as he felt his headache kick in again. The bottle of aspirin was also on the counter. She must have gotten it from the medicine cabinet upstairs.

A slice of memory wove its way in. He'd heard a

sound upstairs, like someone dropping something on the hardwood floor. Or was it behind him? He remembered turning. The falling snow in the doorway. He'd seen a woman's face the instant before he'd felt the blow. Sid's? No.

His pulse jumped.

It hadn't been Sid who'd hit him.

Chapter Sixteen

Laramie had believed Sid. But if there'd been someone else in his house last night, another woman who looked like Sid, then Sid had left out a key part of her story.

The problem was that this morning, in the light of day, he couldn't be sure of what he'd thought he'd seen before taking the blow. Wouldn't Sid have mentioned it if someone else had been there last night before he came to?

He'd quickly checked the security cameras he'd had installed. And hadn't been surprised to find the cameras had been turned off during the burglary. The woman knew how to cover her tracks. That should have given him some assurance that she knew what she was doing going after her father's killers.

His headache had subsided, but he still had a knot on his skull from where someone had nailed him. A mystery woman who looked enough like Sid to fool him? Or Sid herself?

He'd had trouble getting to sleep last night under the weight of what Sid had told him. He reached for his cell phone. Last night, he'd promised to stay out of it. But how could he? If he did and something happened to her—

Sid's number went straight to voice mail.

"It's just me. I was thinking about you this morning." He disconnected knowing there was no reason to ask her to call him. He doubted she would anyway. She'd been pretty clear last night.

Gingerly touching the bump on his head, he tried to remember what exactly he'd seen. He'd barely pocketed his phone when it rang again. He hoped it was Sid.

"It's Dana," his cousin said cheerfully. "I hope I'm not calling too early. I just wanted to remind you that the ball and auction is tonight." He groaned silently, having forgotten about it. "I took the liberty of having them hold three different costumes, but you need to let them know which one you want."

He swore silently. "Thank you," he said.

"I promise you will be glad you went to it," Dana said. "Everyone will be there."

Not everyone, he thought, thinking of Sid.

"I'll go and pick up my costume this morning," he told her.

"See you tonight. Let us know if you need a ride."

He had to smile as he pocketed his phone. There was no one quite like Dana. Whether or not he'd be glad he attended the ball was debatable, but he would go nonetheless because he adored her. Not because he thought for a moment he would enjoy it.

He couldn't get his mind off Sid and what she'd told him last night as he went to pick up his costume for tonight. She was so sure that the four founding members of the Old West Artists Coalition had been involved in her father's death.

They'd apparently stolen the forgeries and trusted one of them to destroy them. He hadn't. At least that was Sid's theory. Now she thought they would turn on each other. Laramie wished he believed that. They'd kept quiet about what they'd done, if Sid was right, for all these years.

It wasn't until later in the day, after running errands, that he turned on the television. He made up his mind that he couldn't sit back and do nothing. He would find out everything he could about the artists she thought were involved, he told himself, as he dressed for the ball.

That's why, when the local news came on, he couldn't have been more shocked. Maybe Sid was right after all.

ROCK JACKSON'S MURDER topped the news. Even more shocking was the arrest of Taylor West.

Laramie stood in front of the television, having a hard time believing what he was hearing. Taylor West had apparently been found passed out in his vehicle outside the Jackson residence, holding what was believed to be the murder weapon.

West had been intoxicated, resisted arrest and was now charged with multiple offenses, including homicide.

"The cowboy artist's death has now been linked to a counterfeit money operation," the broadcaster was saying. "It is uncertain if West was involved in the counterfeit operation with Jackson. But items found at the scene along with that found in a storage unit implicates artist Rock Jackson in the counterfeiting operation."

The broadcaster cut to an interview with Cody Kent and another man identified as cowboy artist Hank Ramsey. He recognized Cody and turned up the volume. Cody was saying he was shocked by the turn of events. He said he hadn't seen either man in some time.

"What a tragedy," Cody said. "Two such talented artists. They'll both be missed."

Hank Ramsey was as dark as Cody Kent was blond. Unlike Cody, he was clean-shaven with his dark hair cut short. He nervously turned the brim of his Stetson while he talked, his voice breaking at times.

"A tragedy. I only know what I heard on the news this morning. I talked to Taylor recently. I knew he was upset, but I never dreamed... Just a tragedy."

The television station cut back to the broadcaster, who moved on to other news. Laramie's phone rang.

"I assume you've seen the news," his brother Austin said.

"Do they know why Taylor West killed him?" Laramie had to ask. His head swam. Did this have something to do with the forgeries?

"I talked to Hud. Apparently Rock was having an affair with Taylor's wife. Taylor swears he didn't kill the man, but his gun appears to be the murder weapon, and he was in possession of it at the time of his arrest. Hud thinks it might also have something to do with the counterfeit money operation. Taylor swears he had nothing to do with that, either."

Laramie thought about telling his brother what had happened at his house last night. But apparently it had nothing to do with the murder or the counterfeit operation. At least he hoped to hell it didn't.

"Glad Hud caught the counterfeiter," he managed to say, wondering if anyone else was involved. And if Taylor West was telling the truth about not killing Rock, then who did?

He tried Sid's number again only to have it go straight to voice mail. He didn't leave a message. As he pocketed the phone, he feared she might be up to her neck in all this.

THE HOLIDAY BALL and Art Auction was held each year at the Big Sky Pavilion. Laramie saw the lights from miles away. Valets parked cars in one of the huge snowy lots above it. Along with arranging for a costume, Dana had made sure that Laramie had his ticket.

She had a one-in-three chance of figuring out who he was, given that she had arranged the costumes. But he wasn't sure what she and Hud would be wearing. His brothers had been equally secretive.

Waiters moved through the crowd with bubbling champagne flutes and fancy hors d'oeuvres. The lobby was a roar of voices. Beyond it, Laramie could hear music playing. He asked one of the waiters about the art that would be auctioned off tonight and was pointed to a door off the ballroom.

The three paintings were displayed under spotlights along one wall. A dozen people milled around the room. A bored-looking older man wearing a jacket that read SECURITY stood in the corner.

Laramie moved in closer to look at the three cowboy paintings. One by Taylor West, one by Rock Jackson and the last by H. F. Powell. As he caught bits of conversation, it appeared that everyone had heard the news tonight. The expectation was that both the West and Jackson paintings' bids would go quite high.

But he realized the real prize in this room was the H. F. Powell painting—if the low murmurs he'd picked up were any indication. There was talk of the painting going for more than a couple hundred thousand, but that it could go even higher because it was one of the few works of the deceased artist anyone had seen in years.

"Excuse me." Laramie addressed a woman who was studying the Powell painting. "I take it H. F. Powell paintings are rare?" he asked, remembering what Sid had told him.

The woman lifted one fine shaped brow. "He was one of the most prolific artists of his time, but he stopped painting a few years before he died." She leaned in closer. "It was rumored that he had personal problems. It was such a tragedy. He was killed in a fire at his studio. A lot of his work was lost in the fire so any painting of his is even more valuable now. This is one I've never seen before."

Interesting, Laramie thought as he studied the Powell painting. It was of a beautiful woman on a galloping horse, a rock-and-pine landscape behind her. The colors were warm as if the day had been, as well. The woman's face was filled with joy. He got the feeling she was riding toward her lover.

He studied it, surprised that not only could he feel the warmth of the day, he could almost smell the dust being kicked up by the horse's hooves. Surprising himself, he also realized he was going to have to bid on the painting. He wanted it like he had never wanted anything before because, given the resemblance, he would swear the woman on the horse was Sid's mother.

He'd never cared that much about material things. But he had to have this painting—no matter what it cost. He just hoped that wasn't what everyone else in the room was thinking, as well.

S<small>ID SPOTTED THE MAN</small> dressed as Zorro standing in front
of the H. F. Powell painting. She had cheated, wait-
ing outside until she'd seen Laramie Cardwell's SUV
pull up. She hadn't wanted to take any chances, but
the truth was she would have recognized him no matter his disguise.

She'd spent her life studying forms as an artist.
Laramie's form was quite fine. As she slipped through
the small crowd standing around the paintings, she realized she would love to paint him. The thought surprised her, since it had been so long since she'd gotten
to paint what she really loved.

Sid could see that Laramie was taken with the H. F.
Powell painting. The painting was one of her father's
best compositions, she thought, as she admired it under
the soft lights highlighting it. Then out of the corner
of her eye, she watched Laramie.

He couldn't seem to take his eyes from the painting. She guessed he had seen the resemblance between
her and her mother. Around her, she heard everyone
talking about the painting, all of them wondering how
high the bidding would go and ultimately, who would
be taking it home.

It saddened her to think that most of her father's
career, this kind of art hadn't been popular. With the
influx of people like the ones in this room with money
and a desire to rediscover the Old Wild West, paintings like this one were now coveted. Too bad he hadn't
lived long enough to see how badly people wanted an
H. F. Powell painting.

But then again, her father had never painted for the
money. And he certainly wouldn't have been caught
dead at an affair like this. She smiled to herself, re-

membering that she'd told Laramie the same thing about herself. She still hoped it was true.

As Laramie moved on to Rock Jackson's painting, Sid stepped closer to the H. F. Powell painting. She stared at it with a mix of emotions. The painting caught her mother's beauty as well as her wild spirit with brushstrokes that spoke of the love the artist had felt for this woman. Her mother had been caught with that excited look in her eyes, that unmasked joy in her face... Until that moment, Sid hadn't felt the emotion captured in the painting. Her mother had been a woman in love.

"It is beautiful, isn't it?" asked a woman on the other side of her. "It moves me to tears, as well." The woman pressed a tissue into Sid's hand as she moved away. Sid hadn't realized she was smiling through her tears.

LARAMIE CAUGHT A WHIFF of perfume in a room full of warring fragrances. But he couldn't be sure that light citrusy scent was what had made him aware of a woman standing in front of the H. F. Powell painting. Maybe he'd just sensed her.

When he looked over at the masked woman, he felt a start. She was dressed in all black, from the old-fashioned hooped-skirt dress to the large floppy hat that hid her hair. She turned her head. He caught only a glimpse of cool blue eyes framed by a dark mask— just as they had been the first time he'd ever laid eyes on her.

It couldn't be Sid. She'd said she wouldn't be caught dead here. And yet this woman was the right height and the right frame from what he could see of her. Her elaborate dress hid her figure and her face was obscured by the hat and mask along with the high neck of the dress.

But it was Obsidian "Sid" Forester. He moved closer, following the faint scent of her perfume. Why had she lied about coming here? Or had her plans changed since the time he'd ask her?

He was next to her now. All his senses told him it was her. But when she raised her lashes to meet his gaze, she gave no indication that she'd ever seen him before.

In the other room, someone announced that the ball was about to begin. Music soared and the crowd began to thin. As the woman in black began to move away, he grabbed her hand. Without looking at her, he whispered, "Dance with me."

He felt her freeze. When his gaze met hers, he saw both surprise and wariness in those beautiful eyes. He tried to hide his own shocked expression. This woman wasn't Sid, not the woman he'd kissed, not the woman he'd dreamed about every night since. But he was convinced that they'd met before. Last night, when she'd put the knot on his head.

He felt her hesitate and started to let go of her hand, when she nodded slowly and did an old-fashioned curtsy. As the crowd began to move toward the ballroom, she said, "If you will excuse me for just a moment…"

Before he could protest, she disappeared into the ladies' room. He waited patiently. A few moments later, she returned. He saw the change instantly and yet he questioned if he was losing his mind as he led her out of the art room, onto the dance floor and into his arms.

Her eyes met his briefly, almost shyly, before she lowered her lashes. He felt his heart cartwheel in his chest. This wasn't the same woman he'd asked to dance.

He glanced around for another woman in black, but didn't see one. What game were they playing with him? Sid moved gracefully in his arms. His cat burglar had been light on her feet. No wonder she was such a graceful dancer. But what was she doing here? Shouldn't she be burglarizing someone else's house right now?

"Enjoying the dance?" he whispered near her ear. He felt her shiver.

"I am," she replied in a whisper that had intrigued him the first time they'd met.

He breathed in the citrus scent of her, reveling in the feel of her in his arms. How badly he wanted to kiss her again, knowing that if he did, there would be no more hiding behind the mask. He would have to demand what she was doing here because all his instincts warned him that she was up to trouble.

But as they danced, he was so happy to have her in his arms that he didn't want it to end. Unfortunately, the song did end, though, and she stepped back. He reached for her, but she slipped from his grasp.

And with a slight shake of her head, she gave him another quick curtsy and disappeared into the crowd.

He thought about going after her, cornering her, unmasking her, but good sense kept him from it. He'd promised to stay out of her business. But what was she up to? He hated to think, as he glanced toward the art room. The door was closed, the older security guard standing in front of it.

When someone touched his shoulder, Laramie jumped.

"Is anything wrong?" his cousin Dana asked him.

Laramie shook his head, but he feared a lot of things were wrong.

"You're the only cousin I haven't danced with tonight," she said.

Laramie was happy to dance with Dana. He understood how she had become the matriarch of the family even at her young age. She'd brought them all together as a family because of her loving nature. Everyone loved Dana.

"Are you having fun?" she asked as they danced.

Fun didn't really describe it, but he nodded and smiled. "I'm glad I'm here," he said truthfully, which made her smile.

"I saw you dancing with a woman dressed all in black," Dana said.

"Did you recognize her?" he asked quickly.

"No." She frowned, looking surprised. "You didn't know who she was, either?" That seemed to amuse her. "That explains why you keep looking for her."

"I'm sorry," he apologized. He hadn't even realized he'd been doing that.

Dana laughed. "I'm just glad to see you enjoying yourself."

When the dance ended, she said, "There are some people I want you to meet." She led him back to the lobby.

For the next half hour, he tried to remember the names of the ranchers, business owners and neighbors Dana introduced him to. More champagne was forced on him as he nodded and smiled and thought about the woman he'd danced with.

It wasn't until someone announced it was almost

time for the partygoers to reveal their identities that he escaped back into the ballroom. He had to find the woman.

He worked his way through the crowd, looking for her.

She'd left, he decided. And yet he'd been in the lobby. He hadn't been so distracted that he wouldn't have noticed if she'd passed him. Was there another way out of here? There would be emergency exits, but those would set off alarms.

Just when he thought he'd only imagined her—or she'd evaporated into thin air—he spotted her. She was coming out of the ladies' room. He hadn't thought that was where she might be. He hesitated, realizing also that she probably hadn't attended the ball alone.

He waited for her to make a beeline for some handsome man. The countdown began. Ten. Nine. Eight. The huge room went quiet as everyone anticipated the unmasking. Except his woman in black. Seven. Six. Five. She seemed to be making a beeline not for some handsome escort, but for the door.

Laramie stepped in front of her. Four. Three. Her gaze flew up to his. He saw the alarm as she tried to step around him. Two. One!

Masks started coming off all around the huge ballroom.

"Please," she said as she tried to get past him.

"It's time to unmask," he said and peeled off his own.

She met his eyes with a steely look. Her eyes had gone from cool blue to silver steel. With an arrogant lift of her head, she reached for her mask.

A blood-curdling scream filled the ballroom, followed by the sound of several people running. Laramie turned to see that the door to the art room was open. Even from where he was standing, he could see that the H. F. Powell painting was gone.

As he turned back, he saw that the painting wasn't the only thing missing. His woman in black was also gone.

Chapter Seventeen

Laramie saw the marshal and his brothers Austin and Hayes heading for the art room and quickly followed. Hud barked out orders to the pavilion guards to have all the doors blocked. No one was to leave. Then he motioned them and the guard in and closed the door.

"This door was locked?" Hud asked the guard the moment they were all in the room.

"I locked it myself."

"And there was no one in the room?"

"No." The guard glanced around the space. "Where would they have hidden?"

It was a good question. The room had been bare except for the paintings. Not a stick of furniture was in the room. Laramie looked toward the windows as Hud walked over to them.

"The windows don't open. Nor are there any footprints in the snow outside them," the marshal said as he turned back to the room. "No other doors in or out."

It must have dawned on them all at the same time, because they all looked up. Hud swore. A piece of the dropped ceiling had been left ajar.

"Seal the room," he said as he reached for his cell phone and barked, "Make sure no one leaves."

"Are you going to detain and question everyone outside this room?" Austin asked. They would be here all night and then some if that was the case.

Hud shook his head irritably. "But I need some men at the door to make sure no one walks out of here with that painting in case the burglar left that ceiling tile like that to misdirect us." He looked from Austin to Hayes and then Laramie. "Mind helping until I can get deputies and a crime-scene team over here?"

Laramie joined his brothers at the pavilion's main entrance. The Powell painting was large enough that it wouldn't fit under most costumes, so screening people as they left went fairly fast.

The whole time, he found himself looking for the woman in black. She didn't come through the lines. Which meant she'd left right after the missing painting was discovered? But Hud had asked that all the doors be covered. Maybe she slipped out before the guards could get to the doors. He thought of her hooped skirt and swore. The Powell painting could have fit under it.

Then he saw her. She had taken off her mask, but still wore the wide-brimmed hat that hid most of her face. Only when she glanced up did he catch the glint of her silvery-blue eyes. Eyes like a wolf, he thought.

She had started toward his line, then looked up and seen him. Hesitating, he saw her look to the other lines.

Something shone in those eyes for a moment. Defiance? Challenge? It must have been, because she stepped into his line. As he checked one after another ball goer through, she moved closer and closer.

It wouldn't be long before she was standing directly in front of him.

Laramie could hear people complaining. Some were threatening to call their lawyers.

He let two more people out and turned to find himself face-to-face with the woman of his nightly dreams and his growing obsession. Her head was down, the hat shadowing her face.

He hoped to hell she didn't think he would let her get out of here with the painting. "I'm going to have one of the women check under your hoop skirt," he said.

"That isn't necessary," she said and lifted the framework of the skirt. She wore black yoga pants beneath the skirt. No painting. When he glanced up at her, he saw the smile and the amusement in her eyes before he jerked back in surprise.

This woman looked like Obsidian "Sid" Forester. They would have been twins…

"Let's keep the lines moving," Hud ordered as the grumbling increased among the waiting guests.

"If that's all…" the woman said. She even sounded like Sid, he thought as he watched the woman who'd coldcocked him last night walk away.

TAYLOR WEST NEEDED a drink like he'd never needed one before. He'd awakened with a killer headache and the worst taste in his mouth. When he'd sat up, it took him a few moments to realize where he was. In jail. For murder.

Stumbling to his feet, he lurched toward the bars.

"Hey!" he yelled and listened for someone to come. No one did. "Hey!"

When a deputy finally did show his face, Taylor said, "I'll pay you to get me a drink."

The deputy shook his head and started to close the door.

"Wait! Do you know who I am? I'm Taylor West. I'll give you any painting you want. Just between you and me."

"You need to quiet down. Try to get some rest." He closed the door and even when Taylor yelled obscenities at his departing form, the deputy didn't return.

He banged on the bars of his cell and yelled, "I didn't murder anyone!"

"Didn't your lawyer tell you not to talk about your case?" asked a voice. Taylor couldn't see the man because they were in separate cells divided by a wall instead of bars.

"What's it to you?" he demanded.

"You should listen to your lawyer."

Taylor scoffed at that. "You know what they say about lawyers? Once you need one, you're already screwed." He wandered over to his bunk and sat down, his head in his hands. He would kill for a drink.

"Who didn't you murder?" the man asked.

"The two-bit artist Rock Jackson."

"I know who Rock is," the voice said. "Why *didn't* you kill him?"

Taylor wasn't about to get into it with a stranger. "He was running around with my wife."

"That can get a man killed, all right."

"I planned to kill him. I was waiting outside his house."

"So what happened?"

Taylor thought of the crime shows he'd seen on television. The incarcerated killer always had a big mouth and talked too much to a jailhouse snitch. "What's it to you?"

"I can't sleep, either."

"What are you in for?"

"Writing hot checks."

"*Hot* checks?"

"Checks you can't make good on because you don't have any money."

"At least I don't have that problem," Taylor said, and they both laughed. "When the cops found me I was passed out in my truck with an empty quart bourbon bottle in one hand and my gun in the other. The last thing I remember before that was closing my eyes to wait for my cheating wife and Rock to return."

"Sounds to me like you were framed."

Framed? He lay back on the bunk, staring up at the stained ceiling. "Who would want to frame me?"

"Good question," the man said. "Have you made anyone mad lately?"

"Who *haven't* I made mad?" Taylor said to himself and closed his eyes. But the list of the people who might want to frame him for murder was short and he'd confided in them about the forged painting.

SID WASN'T SURPRISED when she heard the knock at her door. She glanced at the clock. Almost two in the morning. She'd known she wouldn't be able to sleep, so she hadn't even tried. Instead, she'd been painting. It was what she did when she was upset.

"Your light was on," Laramie said by way of explanation when she opened the door. He glanced past her to the costume from the ball that had been tossed onto a chair. Sid now wore jeans and a T-shirt.

Opening the door wider, she motioned him in with a wave of her hand. After seeing him at the ball, she'd suspected it was only a matter of time before he showed up. What surprised her was that the marshal and a couple of deputies weren't with him.

"I thought you said you wouldn't be caught dead at the ball," he said as she closed the door and turned to look at him. He had stopped in the middle of her living room.

She could tell he was angry. But she suspected he was also scared. "Fortunately I wasn't."

He stepped toward her. "Where is the Powell painting?"

"You don't understand."

"Don't I?" He took another step. "You've been playing some kind of game with me since the first night we met. You're lucky I'm here instead of with the marshal."

"Why isn't the marshal here?"

Another step toward her. The room seemed to be closing in, getting smaller and smaller. She could smell the cold night air on him and remembered the way he'd pulled her close earlier when they'd danced. He was almost that close again.

"Because I wanted to give you the opportunity to level with me. For starters, I know you're in more trouble than you're telling me."

She smiled, holding her ground. "You think you know me?"

He was just inches away now. "I know how you feel in my arms. I know how you taste."

She felt something give in her chest as he reached out and cupped her cheek. She'd tried to forget how his mouth had felt and tasted on hers, how safe she'd felt in his arms, how her heart raced when he was this close.

"You weren't alone at my house last night," Laramie said, his voice little more than a whisper. He was so close she could smell his warm scent. "It was your twin."

"My twin? I don't have—"

"You don't have a sister or cousin or some relative who looks enough like you that you used her tonight to pull off the heist? You want to keep pretending you don't know what I'm talking about?"

She started to step away, needing to put space between them, afraid of what she would do if she didn't.

He grabbed her arm and pulled her into him. His voice was rough, his hands strong. "Tell me what's going on. All that stuff you told me last night? Was it just a crock of crap to keep me out of your hair tonight? Come on, Sid. You're too good at what you do," he said as his gaze swept over the painting on her easel.

She'd known he would figure it out. She'd let him get too close. Her mistake.

Laramie looked from the painting to her. His eyes widened as if the truth had just struck him. "You're not just a master thief. *You're* an art forger."

SID WRENCHED FREE of his grasp and stepped past him and, for a moment, Laramie thought she might be going for a weapon. His head still ached from last night. If he could help it, he wasn't going to let that happen again. He turned to watch her step into the kitchen and open the refrigerator.

"I'll take that as a compliment," she said as she grabbed two bottles of beer. She held one out to him. When he didn't reach for it, she said, "You came here for the truth, right? Now you're not sure you want to hear it."

"Try me. Or we can just call the marshal."

"Which makes me wonder why you haven't called him." She squinted, studying him openly. "Maybe because you have no proof. You cried wolf once, the first night we met. You don't want to do it again with the marshal. Am I right?"

She was. It didn't surprise him that she knew he'd gone to the marshal the first night when he'd caught her coming out of his future house with the painting.

The truth. That was why he'd come here tonight. At least in part. He took one of the beers that she offered. Twisting off the top with both anger and frustration, he took a drink, watching her over the bottle. "What you told me last night—"

"Was all true."

"But you didn't tell me everything."

Sid met his gaze. "I wasn't sure I could trust you."

"Trust *me*?" He laughed as he watched her twist off the bottle cap and toss it into the trash before taking a long drink.

She motioned toward a place for him to sit, but he was too restless. She was right. He wasn't sure he wanted to hear the truth. He'd fallen for this woman— a thief, an apparent forger, a cat burglar.

He stepped into her studio off the living room. The room was small with large windows. Because of the lack of wall space, paintings were stacked against the walls. "You painted all of these?" he asked turning to find her standing in the doorway, holding her beer. She nodded.

"I thought you didn't like cowboy art?"

She said nothing as she took another swig of her beer.

In one corner of the room was a stack of old logging crosscut handsaws. The rusted metal between the handles had Montana scenes painted on them. He noticed at once that they weren't half as good as the paintings. That wasn't all he noticed. Her cowboy art wasn't just good, it was masterful and yet she wasn't in the Old West Artists Coalition—just like her father. Nor had he seen her work in any of the galleries he'd visited.

He stared at one of the paintings for a long moment, something stirring inside him. He could feel her watching him. It came to him like another knock to his head.

Turning quickly, he stared at her. "Tell me I'm wrong about you."

"I wish I could."

"I don't get you."

"I think you do."

He smiled at that and shook his head. "I *want* to. You're obviously talented. *Very* talented. So I ask myself what is she doing painting old saw blades? What is it she's hiding other than her obvious talent?"

She lifted her chin. He'd seen that defiant look on her before. "Now you think you have me all figured out."

"Nope, I suspect it could take a lifetime to do that." He put down his beer and closed the distance between them in two long strides. He took her bottle from her and set it aside as he drew her to him. "The H. F. Powell painting that was stolen tonight? I wanted it more than I have wanted anything. Except," he drawled, "*you*. It was because, on some level, I knew. You painted it. But what about the auction?"

"I couldn't let it be auctioned off as one of my father's paintings. It was stolen from his art studio the night he was killed. One of the members of the OWAC donated it anonymously. The killer knows I'm coming for him. Don't worry. I'll make it right with the charity."

"If you're still alive. Sid, we have to go to the marshal."

"Are you sure we have to go right now?" She looked up at him, her blue eyes bright as diamonds, her lips parting. He dropped his mouth to hers.

Then he swung her up into his arms and carried her to the bedroom just off the studio.

SID LOOKED INTO his eyes as he gently laid her on the bed. His expression made her weak inside. His touch was so tender as he crawled onto the bed next to her and drew her close again. He dropped his mouth to hers, exploring her intimately as if there was still so much he wanted to know about her.

She felt the same way. As he drew back from the passionate kiss, he traced his thumb over her lower lip.

"I fell in love with your mouth that night," he said quietly. As he lifted his gaze, he said, "And your eyes. You have the most incredible eyes. I feel as if I can look into your soul."

Sid shivered. "Don't look too closely."

He shook his head. "You're not as bad as you want me to believe," he said just as quietly. "What do you see when you look into my eyes?"

"Kindness, compassion…" She halted seeing something that tied her tongue in a knot for a moment. "Caring."

He smiled. "Caring? Look deeper."

She let out a nervous laugh even as she was filled with pure joy. "Love?"

Laramie nodded. "I've fallen for you, Obsidian Forester. Fallen hard."

Sid couldn't speak, which was just as well because in the next moment he stole her breath away as he cupped her face in his big hands and kissed her again.

She felt wrapped in wisps of soft, warm clouds as he began to unbutton her shirt. His fingers brushed over the tops of her breasts, hardened her nipples to aching pebbles. He followed his fingers with his mouth, suckling at her until she cried out with a desire that burned to the heart of her.

With fumbling fingers, she helped him remove her own and his clothing. She sighed at the feel of his naked skin, the taut muscles of his chest and arms and stomach. Wrapping her arms around him, she pulled him to her.

When they came together it was as if they had been missing pieces of a puzzle that finally had found each other. They moved with the ancient rhythm of passion and love.

Sid arched against him, crying out when he brought her to the peak of desire, and she shuddered in his arms as she collapsed on the bed. The cool night air moved over her perspiring bare skin like a caress.

They might have stayed like that the rest of the night—if it hadn't been for the back door banging open.

Chapter Eighteen

Laramie sat up with a start, grabbing for his jeans as heavy footfalls could be heard from the other room. He glanced at Sid, her face pale and worried in the soft glow coming through the window. From her expression, she had no idea who had just broken into her cabin.

She was reaching for her robe and he'd only managed to drag on his jeans and button all but the top button when a figure filled the doorway, a second larger figure behind it.

The overhead light came on, momentarily blinding him.

"Sorry, it wasn't my idea to come barging in," a woman said. Laramie did a double take at her—and the armed masked man holding the gun to the woman's head.

"What have you done now, Zander?" Sid demanded as she pulled on her robe and tied the sash tight around her middle.

The woman who was the spitting image of Sid shrugged. "You know me, sis. Trouble just seems to find me. But this time I have a feeling this is more about you than me."

"She *is* your sister," Laramie said as he realized this

had been the woman who'd knocked him out the previous night at his house.

"*Half* sister," Zander said and smiled. "The bad half, if you ask Sid."

"Enough. Give me the paintings," the man said. "All of them, including the one you stole tonight, or I kill her."

"I don't think so," Sid said.

Laramie recognized the man's voice. Cody Kent. "You'd better listen to him, Sid. If you're right, he's already killed once. Isn't that right, Cody? You killed H. F. Powell the night you stole the paintings."

"What?" the artist was clearly taken aback. "I didn't kill Powell." He ripped off the ski mask as he shoved Zander into the room. Waving the gun, he said, "Just give me the paintings and no one gets hurt."

"Is that what you told our father?" Sid demanded.

"*Your father*?" Cody asked in confusion. "I didn't think H.F. had any family."

"He didn't have much regard for marriage," Zander said with a sigh. "But, like his daughters, he believed in justice. He planned to nail you and the others to the wall. He would have shown you all up and you knew it."

Cody waved the gun at them. "Look, we just went to his studio to talk to the crazy old coot. No one was supposed to get hurt. But H.F. was determined to ruin us all and destroy everything we'd built with the coalition. We didn't even believe he'd forged our paintings until we entered the studio and saw them."

Sid made a disparaging sound. "But once you did, you couldn't let the public see them. Were you afraid that if you just took them, he would only repaint them? He wasn't a man easily persuaded."

Cody swore. "I saw that we were getting nowhere with him, I wanted to leave. But we weren't leaving without the forgeries. H.F. put up a fight, but finally he gave in. We carried the paintings to the car."

"Including the one that was up for auction tonight," Laramie said.

"That was Rock. He had to have it. We tried to talk him out of it, but he wouldn't listen," Cody said.

"So how did you end up with all of the paintings?" Sid asked.

The artist looked surprised. "What makes you think—"

"You're the one standing here with the gun," she said.

Cody chuckled. "Rock promised to get rid of the forgeries, but I didn't trust him. I was right. I discovered where he'd hidden them. That's why he couldn't tell anyone when he discovered they were missing."

Laramie wanted to rush the man, but he couldn't take the chance that Cody wouldn't get off a shot. In the small cabin, it would be too easy to wound or kill one of them.

"Why didn't *you* destroy them?" Laramie asked.

Cody shook his head. "They were beautiful." He looked at Sid. "Your father was the most talented artist I've ever met. He was brilliant. Crazy as a loon, but a real genius. I knew I should destroy them, but I couldn't. After a few years, I sold them. They were worth a lot more by then because our careers were going better. I figured the chances were good no one would ever find out."

"It wasn't easy, but I found them," Sid said.

He didn't seem to hear her. "Once I saw the one you brought to the gallery, I pretended to be as upset as Taylor was," he said to Laramie. "We were all trying to get ahold of Rock. I knew he'd admit that they'd been stolen from him, but no one would believe him. But I had bigger problems. There was talk of a cat burglar in Big Sky. Only this cat burglar didn't take anything. I paid a couple of houses a visit and realized quickly what was going on when I saw some of the originals H.F. had used to make his forgeries."

"Is that when you panicked and anonymously donated what you thought was an H. F. Powell painting to the auction? That painting was a new one still on the easel in his studio the night he was killed."

"You have no idea how hard it was to part with it," Cody said. "That painting is worth a small fortune."

Sid shook her head. "It would be—if my father had painted it. During the last years of his life, H.F. quit painting his own art to make forgeries of all your work. To keep the creditors at bay and the three of us fed, I painted in my father's style."

"It was a *forgery*?" Cody let out a bitter curse. "You're just a family of forgers."

"Exactly," Zander said. "Our family was all smoke and mirrors."

Cody looked sick. "I knew someone was switching the real paintings and collecting the forgeries once I heard about the so-called cat burglar. I just didn't know who until tonight. I thought you would try to steal the painting. But I didn't know how you would do it. Imagine my shock when I saw you in that black dress jumping down off the roof with it. I planned to follow you, but you got away. I thought I'd blown it, then low and behold, I spotted your double and she led me right to you."

"Hank Ramsey was in on it, too, right?" Laramie asked. "Why isn't he here?"

"I stopped by his place tonight." Cody sighed. "I found him hanging from a beam in his kitchen."

"You might as well put down the gun," Laramie said. "It's all going to come out now."

Cody shook his head. He looked broken, like a man who had nothing to lose. "My art is all I have. Destroy that and I have nothing." He leveled the gun at Sid. "No matter what happens to me, those forgeries have to be destroyed." He pulled a bottle from his coat pocket. Laramie recognized it for what it was. A homemade firebomb—probably like the one he had used the night of H. F. Powell's studio fire.

SID HAD BEEN watching everything play out in front of her, feeling a little dazed. Since her father's death, she'd been grieving for all that had been lost. Once the first forgery had turned up, she'd been on a mission to catch her father's killer.

Cody Kent. She'd known it would be one of the original cowboy artists who started the coalition—or all four of them. She'd just never guessed it would be Cody who showed up at her door.

Laramie took a step toward Cody. She could tell he was trying to gauge his chances. He had to know that there was no one more dangerous than a man backed into a corner.

Sid stepped in front of Laramie. Her heart broke at the thought that she might get him killed over all this.

If only she hadn't gotten him involved. Zander, as well. She was going to get them all killed, and for what? Some artist's ego? Or the price of an artist's reputation?

"I didn't want it to be you," Sid said to Cody. "I guess we all wanted to believe it was Rock Jackson. But when I heard the news, I wondered why Rock would be making counterfeit money if he was the one who'd been selling the paintings he'd stolen from my father that night."

Cody nodded, a bitter smile coming to his lips. "I realized that something like this could happen. That some fool might take H.F.'s copy of one of the paintings to an expert. I wasn't stupid."

"So why sell them?" Laramie asked.

Cody shrugged. "In retrospect, I should have destroyed them."

Sid shook her head. "If Rock had already taken the forgeries that night…you didn't have to go back and kill my father. H.F. was old and tired. He wouldn't have redone the forgeries. But you couldn't let him show you up. It was more about your pride, your ego, than the paintings or even what the organization had been doing. By then, I'm sure your group had covered up the charity scam." She glanced at the glass jar clutched in his hand. "You went there to end it once and for all."

"I thought I could talk some sense into the old fool." Cody shook his head. "It's all water under the bridge now, though. There won't be anyone left who will be able to say differently and the forgeries will be destroyed for good."

"What about Taylor?" Laramie demanded, moving up beside Sid, determined to protect her. How she loved this gallant man. "Taylor's going to sing like a canary. He'll tell everything he knows."

"Even if anyone believed a word he said now that he's facing a murder charge, Taylor doesn't know anything," Cody said.

"That's too bad because I'm betting he didn't kill Rock," Laramie said. "Or that Hank Ramsey didn't hang himself, either."

"If you're expecting a confession…" Cody said as he took a step back.

"You toss that in here and you'll never get out in time to save yourself," Sid said seeing him look toward a candle that still burned next to the bed. "I don't think you've thought this through. Also you will destroy some of my father's paintings. Thanks to you, they're worth more now than when he was alive." He hadn't been able to destroy the forgeries. He wouldn't be able to burn her father's originals. "Not to mention…" She looked toward the bank of windows in the studio.

Cody looked angry and upset as he followed her gaze. He realized as she had that the windows were large enough that at least one of them might be able to get out before the fire killed them.

"Thank you for pointing that out," he said. At gunpoint, he forced them all into a windowless storage room at the back of the cabin where Sid kept the old saws and milk cans she'd collected for her crafts.

"I'm sorry you have to die," Cody said. "You have your father's talent. But you also don't follow the rules. You could never be a member of the Old West Artists Coalition."

Laramie balled up his fist and took a step forward, but Sid caught his arm as Cody retreated from the room, slamming the door behind him and pitching them into darkness. Sid heard him lock the door and shove what sounded like her heavy buffet in front of it.

Chapter Nineteen

Laramie snapped on the switch he'd seen by the door. The small storage room was suddenly illuminated by a dim bulb hanging from the ceiling. He turned to Sid. "Tell me there is a reason you wanted him to trap us in here."

"Other than my sister is as crazy as our father and is determined to get us all killed?" Zander asked.

Sid stepped to the door, putting her ear against it. "Just as I thought, he's looking for the forgeries and stealing some of my paintings. I'm just thankful Cody appreciates good art. Now that he knows I'm H.F.'s daughter…he probably figures they'll be worth a lot of money once I'm dead." Her lips turned up in a knowing yet bitter smile. Then she quickly turned toward the old metal milk cans stacked in a corner. "Help me move these as quietly as we can."

"See what I mean? Crazy, just like our father," Zander said. Laramie thought the last thing Sid had done was lose her mind, so he hurried to help her and saw what had been hidden under the milk cans—a hatch in the floor.

He moved quickly to lift it. A blast of freezing cold

air rose with the door. He looked down at the steps that disappeared into the darkness. "An escape tunnel?"

Zander laughed as her sister handed her a flashlight. "So this is where you hid the forgeries."

"Quickly," Laramie said as Zander snapped on the light and began to climb down. "We have to get out of here before he sets the place on fire." He looked at Sid. "If he burns the cabin, your work will go up in flames."

She smiled almost sadly and descended the stairs.

Laramie followed on her heels. They moved through a long tunnel that ended with a set of crude steps that went up.

"This is that other cabin in the woods," Zander said as they climbed up into a small laundry room lit with daylight coming through the windows.

The moment they stepped out of that room into a larger one, Laramie saw the paintings. Along with the forgeries, he saw dozens of Sid's. Still, he couldn't imagine letting Cody Kent destroy even one of her works.

"Alert the authorities," he said as he headed for the door.

"It's already been done," Sid said. "The moment the hatch was opened an alarm was set off. I have a friend who works at the security company. Wait, where are you going?"

"I can't let him destroy your paintings, let alone get away."

"They aren't worth dying over. I can paint more," she said grabbing at his sleeve. "Neither is catching Cody."

Laramie heard sirens in the distance. "Stay here with your sister." With that, he rushed out the door into the snowy morning.

Chapter Twenty

Sid quickly changed into the clothing she also kept in the second cabin. She'd tried to be prepared for anything that might happen. What she hadn't seen coming was Laramie Cardwell.

"Stay here," she said to Zander as she opened the door to follow Laramie.

"Like that is going to happen," Zander said, right behind her.

Sid couldn't see Laramie as she rushed down the steps and started through the snow-laden pines toward her cabin. One of the reasons she'd bought the property was the tunnel between the two cabins. The owner had told her the tunnel had been dug back in the fifties as a bomb shelter when nuclear war had seemed imminent. The owner had kept the tunnel maintained.

It had saved them temporarily and given her a place to stash the forgeries as well as the bulk of her paintings.

Snow began to fall. At first it was only a few flakes drifting past on the breeze. Then a flurry of them whirled around them as they hurried toward the cabin obscured by trees and snow. Sid could hear sirens com-

ing up the mountain, but feared they would never get
there in time. Laramie had the advantage, she told herself. Cody would be busy trying to make his escape.
But he was greedy. He would also try to pack up as
many of the paintings as he could before he realized
the forgeries weren't there and burned the cabin.

The cabin was old. It would burn quickly. Had they
still been locked in the storage room, she doubted any
of them would have survived.

Ahead, she could see the cabin. Cody had come by
snowmobile, forcing Zander along. It was still sitting
out front. There was no sign of either Cody or Laramie through the pines.

"Shouldn't one of us have a plan?" Zander said behind her.

She saw that her sister had picked up a limb from
the snow. It was thick enough that it could make a
pretty good dent in Cody's head—if Zander got the
chance to use it.

They slowed as they approached the cabin. "I have a
gun just inside the back door in the wicker basket with
my scarves and gloves," Sid whispered. "It's loaded.
So if something happens—"

"I've got you covered, sis."

LARAMIE SPOTTED THE snowmobile sitting outside the
cabin with a half dozen paintings leaning against it.
Sid had been right. The bastard couldn't pass up stealing even more paintings. He treasured them more than
the lives he'd planned to snuff out in the storage room.

Laramie moved cautiously along the side of the
cabin. He could hear Cody inside ransacking the place,

no doubt looking for the forgeries. Which meant that he'd have had to put down the firebomb he'd made.

As he neared the open doorway of the cabin, Laramie peered inside. He couldn't see Cody, but he could hear him. Stepping in, he made his way to the fireplace where the poker leaned against the stone chimney.

"What the hell?" Cody swore as he came out of Sid's studio. He held a painting in both hands. "How did you...?" The rest of his words were lost as he realized that the tables had turned. He threw the painting he'd been holding at Laramie and reached into his pocket for the gun.

From the confused look on his face, Laramie realized that Cody must have laid down the gun somewhere—just as he had the firebomb.

As Cody looked around wildly for both weapons, Laramie spotted the gun lying on the kitchen table about the same time that Cody did. Cody dived for it. Laramie charged. He caught the artist in the back with the poker. Cody let out a loud grunt and staggered, but he didn't go down. Instead, he lurched toward the gun, his fingers within inches of it when Laramie again swung the poker.

This time it caught him in the side of the head. The sound of sirens filled the air as Cody dropped to his knees. Laramie quickly stepped around him and pushed the gun out of the artist's reach.

"You don't understand. That crazy old fool was going to ruin me," Cody said.

Laramie spotted the homemade turpentine firebomb on the kitchen counter where Cody had left it as Sid and Zander rushed in, with Marshal Hud Savage and his deputies on their heels.

THE NEWS HIT the canyon as if it were Cody's firebomb. Cody Kent had been arrested. The homemade turpentine firebomb and Cody's gun had been taken as evidence. Trapped, Cody had broken down and told the authorities everything. He confessed to killing H. F. Powell after the man had tried to destroy his career. After that, he'd confessed to killing Rock and trying to frame Taylor and making Hank Ramsey's death look like a suicide.

The broadcaster was saying, "H. F. Powell's story is one of madness and genius. When he was denied membership in the organization, Old West Artists Coalition, he swore retribution, which ultimately led to his murder. And Cody Kent would have gotten away with it if not for Powell's daughter, Obsidian Forester."

Sid got up to turn off the news as, on screen, Cody was being led into the courthouse. "You don't understand," he told reporters. "All I have is my art."

"Maybe he'll teach an art class in prison," Zander said as Sid turned off the television.

"Maybe," she agreed and looked at Laramie who was frowning at the television. "Is something wrong?" she asked him.

"Just a little confused," he admitted. "If all the paintings but the ones that were stolen burned in the fire…"

"The originals my father copied from were in a safe at the house," Sid said. "He planned to expose the artists at their annual conference, which was to be held here in Big Sky a few days after his death. More than likely our father bragged to someone about what he was going to do."

"Not all of the originals were in the safe," Zander

said, shooting a look at her sister. "What Sid isn't telling you is that her sister stole several of the paintings from the safe and she had to buy them back before she could replace the forgeries." Zander smiled sheepishly at Sid. "I'm sorry I made things harder for you. Because of me, we lost the family ranch."

Sid shook her head. "Dad was so in debt by the time he died, there wouldn't have been a way to save it anyway. You were right. This…quest I've been on… I should have let it go, but I wanted justice and I hated the idea of everyone believing he was so crazy he would kill himself."

"He *was* crazy," Zander said and laughed. "We should know. We're his daughters and the apple doesn't fall far from the tree."

"Well, your father has justice now," Laramie said. "And his daughters have found their way back to each other. I'd say you accomplished more than you set out to." He rose to leave. "The invitation is still open for Christmas Eve at Cardwell Ranch. Open to both of you," he said to Zander.

"So what now?" Zander asked after Laramie left. "You don't have a murderer to catch, no houses to break into… What will my little sis do to keep herself busy?"

"Wipe that grin off your face, Z," she said playfully.

"He's in love with you, you know."

Sid said nothing. She still couldn't believe it. She loved Laramie as well, but their lives were in different states. "He's going back to Houston after the holidays."

Zander lifted a brow. "So go with him."

She shook her head. "My life is here."

"Painting cowboy art." Her sister shook her head

and laughed. "I thought Dad messed *me* up, but he really did a number on you."

"We can't spend the rest of our lives blaming H.F. for our choices," Sid said.

"Maybe you can't," Zander said with a laugh. "But I can. I'm just like him. I'll never settle down."

"Don't say never. Who knows what the future holds."

Her sister seemed to study her for a long moment. "This is the most contented I've ever seen you. Those years when you worked so hard to keep a roof over our heads when Dad had locked himself in his studio and refused to paint his own work and support us... You always did what you had to do."

Sid wished she could believe that. "I forged his work while he was forging others'. You're right. We really *are* messed up, huh?"

Zander smiled. "The ironic thing about all of it? You're a better artist than even the great H. F. Powell." She held up her hand to keep Sid from arguing the point. "It's true, sis. That painting..." She pointed to the one of Sid's mother on horseback that Cody had stolen from her father's studio. "It's a masterpiece. It would have sold for a fortune."

She heard the wistfulness as well as the larceny in her sister's voice.

"We could have both retired on that money," Zander continued. "Instead, you had to give up one of the real H. F. Powells you managed to keep me from stealing to keep us from going to prison."

Sid chuckled. "I don't want to retire. I want to paint. What about you? You have our father's gift, as well."

"Gift? More like a curse." Zander shook her head.

"No, you couldn't make me paint even at gunpoint. I've always hated it. Maybe because it takes practice and I don't care enough to hone my skills. I'll leave art to you. Anyway, look what Cody's artist talent did for him." She stood and reached for her bag. "The difference is that you have more than your art. You have a chance for real happiness with Laramie Cardwell."

"Wait a minute, where are you going? It's Christmas Eve. You said we were going to—"

"We're going to Cardwell Ranch."

"I already told Laramie that we were spending Christmas Eve here," Sid said.

"Well, there's been a change of plans. He invited us both to a real Christmas celebration," Zander said. "It sounds incredibly cheesy, but I'm not about to let you miss that. Come on."

"Are you sure, Z? Hot chocolate, tree trimming, carols around the fire?"

Zander put her arm around her sister. "I can stand it for one night. There will be presents, though, right?"

Sid shook her head at her sister. "I really am glad you came here for Christmas."

LARAMIE HADN'T REALIZED he'd been watching for her until he saw the SUV pull up out front of the ranch house.

Dana grinned at him as he headed out to the porch. It had been a crazy time after the ball, but his cousin was determined that they would have their Christmas Eve come hell or high water.

"Invite Sid and her sister," she'd insisted. "The more the merrier."

"She's having Christmas with her sister at the cabin,"

he'd told his cousin. "It's just as well. I don't see how anything can come of this. I live in Houston. Sid has her own life here."

"You can't see any way to overcome that obstacle?" Dana had asked in exasperation.

"It's more than the fact that our lives are thousands of miles apart," he'd said. "We don't really know each other."

His cousin had given him an impatient look. "You don't believe that any more than I do. And even if it is the case, surely there is some way you can rectify it. Is Houston really calling you back? Or are you just like your brothers were and afraid of giving away your heart?"

Laramie had smiled at Dana. "You just can't stand one of your cousins making a clean getaway."

She'd looked as if she might cry. "No, I can't. Nor do I want Sid to get away. Look what she did to try to bring her father's killer to justice. She risked her life and her reputation and prison."

Fortunately, once the Holiday Masquerade Ball and Auction committee members had learned how it was that the H. F. Powell painting was a forgery and Sid had offered them a real Powell to replace it, they'd dropped any legal charges. Also, Sid had promised to donate one of her paintings for the auction next year. Her paintings were now sought after as much as her father's had been.

"Hello," Laramie called from the porch as Sid and her sister climbed out of the SUV. "Glad to see changed your mind."

"I changed it for her," Zander said.

He smiled. "That was nice of you." As th

the steps, Zander went on past, letting him pull Sid in for quick kiss. "Merry Christmas."

SID STEPPED INTO his arms as if it was the most natural thing. She parted her lips for his warm, sweet kiss and could have stayed in that very spot forever.

At the door, Zander cleared her throat and said, "The kids are watching you two."

They turned, laughing, to see all of the Cardwell brood at the window, hands cupped around their eyes, making faces and laughing.

"Must be time to go in," Sid said, straightening her coat and bracing herself to meet the rest of the family.

Later, Sid sat listening to the sound of a family at play. It was loud and unruly and wonderful.

"Are you doing all right?" Laramie whispered next to her.

She nodded and smiled. "This is normal?"

He laughed. "As normal as the Cardwells get."

"I love it." She'd met his brothers, their wives, Dana's sister and two brothers and their mates, along with Dana's father, Laramie and his brothers' father and mother and his mother's new husband and all the children. There was also Dana's best friend, Hilde, and her husband, a local deputy.

It was insane. The air was filled with noise and the smells of holiday food. There'd been eggnog and hot chocolate and gingerbread men just as she'd predicted...and homemade fudge.

When it got late, the children were put to bed. The finishing touches were put on the tree. Sid had expected a huge, beautiful pine. Instead, it was a large tree.

"Dana can't stand the idea of an ugly tree not getting to be a Christmas tree," her husband the marshal explained with a shake of his head. "We do what we can for it."

When the lights came on, the tree was transformed. As the fire crackled they gathered to sing "Silent Night." Laramie put his arm around her shoulders and pulled her close. She stared at the sparkling lights of the tree and reached for her sister's hand.

"This is the best Christmas I've ever had," she whispered when the song ended.

"It's only the first of many if I have anything to say about it," Laramie told her as he drew her into his arms. "I'm not letting you get away from me again."

From the opposite side of the room, Dana gave him a wink.

* * * * *

INTRIGUE

Available January 19, 2016

#1617 SCENE OF THE CRIME: WHO KILLED SHELLY SINCLAIR?
by Carla Cassidy

Sheriff Olivia Bradford's assigned to clean up corruption in Lost Lagoon. The last person she expects as deputy sheriff is Daniel Carson, a man she'd shared a night with five years before—her daughter's father...

#1618 BLUE RIDGE RICOCHET
The Gates: Most Wanted • by Paula Graves

Undercover agent Nicki Jamison and a wanted FBI staffer, Dallas Cole, must work together to bring down a dangerous militia group. When Nicki is abducted, Dallas will do anything to be reunited with her and her irresistible charm.

#1619 BULLETPROOF BADGE
Texas Rangers: Elite Troop • by Angi Morgan

Undercover Texas Ranger Garrison Travis vows to protect witness Kenderly Tyler from Mafia assassins while clearing himself of murder charges. On the run, they find more than adrenaline pulsing between them, but can they actually make it out alive?

#1620 FULLY COMMITTED
Omega Sector: Critical Response • by Janie Crouch

Agent Jon Hatton's best chance to catch a serial rapist is forensic artist Sherry Mitchell. Jon knows Sherry's determined to help catch this criminal, but keeping her safe is his priority. Followed by making her his bride.

#1621 COLORADO WILDFIRE • by Cassie Miles

Presumed dead, Wade Calloway has returned to the only person who can help him take down a dangerous cartel, Sheriff Samantha Calloway—his wife. If they can finish his assignment, they just might find a fresh start.

#1622 SUSPECT WITNESS • by Ryshia Kennie

A witness to murder, Erin Argon threatens a biker gang's deadly secret. She flees to foreign shores, where CIA agent Josh Sedovich finds her, but can he alone keep her safe?

HICNM0116

SPECIAL EXCERPT FROM

⊕HARLEQUIN®

I N T R I G U E

*When she practically runs over a missing man with
a suspicious reputation on a dark mountain road, an
undercover agent must decide if she can trust he's as
innocent as he claims.*

Read on for a sneak preview of
BLUE RIDGE RICOCHET, the second book in
Paula Graves's heartstopping trilogy
THE GATES: MOST WANTED.

He didn't know how to deal with someone who didn't
seem to want—or need—one damn thing from him.
Especially after the ordeal of the past few weeks. He
didn't know how to relax anymore, how to sit quietly and
eat a bowl of soup without waiting for the next blow, the
next trick.

He knew his name was Dallas Logan Cole. He was
thirty-three years old and had spent the first eighteen years
of his life in Kentucky coal country, trying like hell to get
out before he was stuck there for the rest of his sorry life.
He was a good artist and an ever better designer, and he'd
spent the bulk of his college years trying to leave the last
vestiges of his mountain upbringing behind so he could
start a whole new life.

And here he was, back in the hills, running for his life
again. How the hell had he let this happen?

"I guess those are the only clothes you have?"

He looked down at his grimy shirt and jeans. They
weren't the clothes he'd been wearing when a group of

men in pickup trucks had run his car off the road a few miles north of Ruckersville, Virginia. The wreck had left him a little woozy and helpless to fight the four burly mountain men who'd hauled him into one of the trucks and driven him into the hills. They'd stripped him out of his suit and made him dress in the middle of the woods in the frigid cold while they watched with hawk-sharp eyes for any sign of rebellion.

Rebellion, he'd later learned, was the quickest way to earn a little extra pain.

"It's all I have," he said, swallowing enough humiliating memories to last a lifetime. "Don't suppose you have anything my size?"

Her lips quirked again, triggering a pair of dimples in her cheeks. "Not on purpose. I can wash those for you, though."

"I'd appreciate that." He was finally warm, he realized with some surprise. Not a shiver in sight. He'd begun to wonder if he'd ever feel truly warm again.

She picked up his empty bowl and took it to the sink. "The bathroom's down the hall to the right. Leave your clothes in the hall and I'll put them on to wash."

"And then what?"

She turned as if surprised by the question. "And then we go to bed."

Don't miss
BLUE RIDGE RICOCHET by Paula Graves,
available February 2016 wherever
Harlequin® Intrigue books and ebooks are sold.

www.Harlequin.com